THE MARCH OF THE LONG SHADOWS

Norman Lewis was born in the North London suburb of Enfield. He was written twelve novels and seven non-fiction works. *A Dragon Apparent* and *Golden Earth* are considered classics of travel, and *Naples '44* has been described as one of the ten outstanding books about the Second World War. His most recent work, *The Missionaries*, was published in 1988 to universal acclaim.

ALSO IN ARENA BY NORMAN LEWIS

The Volcanoes Above Us

Norman Lewis

THE MARCH OF THE LONG SHADOWS

ARENA

An Arena Book
Published by Arrow Books Limited
62-65 Chandos Place, London WC2N 4NW

An imprint of Century Hutchinson Limited

London Melbourne Sydney Auckland
Johannesburg and agencies throughout
the world

First published in Great Britain by
Martin Secker & Warburg Limited 1987
Arena edition 1989

Printed and bound in Great Britain by
The Guernsey Press Co. Ltd., Guernsey, Channel Islands.

ISBN 0 09 960530 9

All the languages and major dialects of Europe but one share the saying, 'where there's life there's hope'. The exception is the Sicilian dialect, which on the contrary asserts, 'where there's death there's hope' (*finchè c'è mort c'è speranza*). This unique dissent may typify certain aspects of the island character.

1

THE PEOPLE OF Palma di Cava were set apart from their neighbours in this country by their behaviour when spring hurled itself upon them, like a tiger from cover, some time towards the end of March. No date was fixed for the supposedly pagan rites accompanying its advent. In the middle of the month the farmers would set out clay whistles in grotesque human and animal shapes in their fields. Eventually when the cutting winds from the mountains died away and the *libeccio* gusting from the warm Tyrrhenian sea indicated that rain was on its way, the whistles blew and the seeds went in.

This was the signal for the March of the Long Shadows to take place. At about six in the evening all citizens of any standing lined up in a dishevelled square in the town's western outskirts and walked down a long narrow street to its centre. Men who had done their best to sleep the winter through were awakened to purpose once more, seemingly in some way abetted in new-found resolve by their enormously long and menacing shadows projected by the sun low in the sky at their backs. Beyond the thin encrustation of houses donkeys brayed in their convulsive, ecstatic fashion in open country, and the marchers listened in silent satisfaction to these and such sounds as the screaming of peacocks, equally appropriate to the season. Watching from the wings, as I had done on two previous years, I noted for inclusion in my eventual report: 'For three months life had remained in suspense. All decisions and action have been postponed until this moment. Whatever is to happen, we shall soon know.'

The goal of the walk was a medieval cellar under the Town Hall, and in this the so-called misfits had been assembled for a 'dance', under encouragement or coercion to unleash the mysterious compulsions so often concealed in misshapen bodies, and held locally to benefit the fecundity of nature. It was a religious occasion and apart from the rancidity of excited bodies, the gathering was scented with piety. When all was ready and chalices of strong wine had been emptied by the participants, a three-piece orchestra struck up a tango, and the handicapped couples fell or were shoved into each other's arms. In due course minor palsies and curvatures of the spine were overcome and the misfits performed their annual service for the community, inspiring by passions made voracious by rejection a sympathetic reaction in nature itself. Custom sanctions all. Among a few notabilities present at this scene – from which outsiders were rigorously excluded – was the Archpriest himself who, after the acolytes had sprinkled water, signed with raised fingers the blessing of the Church before the party withdrew.

Primeval irrationalities such as these intertwined with the hard-headed politics of the day would require explanation to the Colonel, whose face, as I had seen him watching from his office window the last of the wartime sheep nudging each other across Regent's Park, had gone a little out of focus in my mind. Strangely I could better remember the carved Indian demon capering above his head.

The meeting had to do with the outrageous possibility of our taking control of Sicily with the support of its separatists. I was to go there and report on progress.

'Likely to be any difficulty about picking up your old contacts once again?' the Colonel asked.

'None whatever.'

'And do you think our Sicilian friends would enjoy being in the Empire?'

'They'd be indifferent.'

He was instantly crestfallen.

'Despite the long historical association – our support for the Bourbons – Nelson?'

'Nothing counts for anything but immediate tangible benefits.'

'The separatists have exerted a good deal of pressure in London as well as in Washington. A Sicilian prince was a guest at Buckingham Palace. I met him. Rather wonderful and scandalous. Truman is said to take them very seriously. Do you think our allies have more to offer?'

'They are richer, and they are further away and thus more easily manipulated.'

'Worldly wisdom seems to me so sad,' he said. There was a foolish and innocent nobility about him. A man who wanted to believe. He had taken time off from the army for a few days at the height of the Chittagong campaign to have his naked body smeared with crimson unguents before symbolical rebirth through the *yoni* of an artificial cow.

'The thing is, can they bring it off?' he asked.

'Everything depends on outside circumstances. For example the strikes could get out of control, or they might find themselves with a peasant revolt on their hands. In this case the people as a whole might well turn to us.'

'Or to our American friends.'

'More likely to them.'

I did my best to keep out of sight for the first hours of the first day, settling myself inconspicuously at a table outside the side-entrance to the Roma, where I had put up for the night, in the Street of the Divine Face which was little frequented, largely because it contained the town morgue. The journey over the ruined roads from Palermo had been exhausting, and this was to be a quiet prelude to the round of visits to my old friends.

Sipping the bitter coffee I watched the street through polygons of misted sunshine. Political posters uncurled like old skin from the shadowed wall across the way. The sky was full of church domes and doves, and a severe-faced old man wearing a cocked hat of the Napoleonic period rode by on a white horse. Beyond and above all, the volcano fumed endlessly.

'How do you unearth your contacts?' the Colonel had asked, a little uneasily, as if nervous of prying into the secrets of a neighbour's closet.

'I make friends,' I told him simply. 'Priests, harlots, waiters. All categories of humanity. People who are obliged to be good listeners. Lonely people who spread rumours. Sometimes there's fire where there's smoke.'

At this moment the Roma's head waiter, Giovanni, a notable collector and disburser of rumour, came into sight, crabbed and hunched in greenish-black, his shoulders permanently frosted with dandruff. I was pleased and a little flattered that he had remembered me and I beckoned him over again and offered him a Lucky Strike cigarette – most prized of all the petty inducements of the black market – which he accepted with gratitude before dropping into the vacant chair. 'Kiss your hand,' he said mechanically in the servile style of the local dialect. 'Your honour, what's the point of hiding yourself away round the corner? Why not sit with the rest of the lordships in the square?'

'I'm resting up after a bit of a journey,' I explained.

'Here for the march?' he asked.

'I saw it.'

'It went off well. At any other time this could have been a good year.'

'But this year it won't?'

'How can it be? Let's be frank. Sicily's screwed. The Allies screwed us. They went off and left us to get on with it. Two years of peace and we're worse off than we were in the war.'

'Food shortages?'

'Take a look round, and you'll find that all the cats have vanished from the streets. Does that strike you as sinister?'

'Unemployment still bad?'

'Worse by far. Speaking for myself, that's hardly a problem. I start at six a.m. and finish at ten at night. Sixteen hours a day to keep the soup flowing for a dozen people. What with kids and grandchildren and half the time with the walls of their stomachs sticking together.'

A thirteen-year-old under-waiter I recognized staggered into sight through the side door carrying a bin of kitchen refuse which he showered into the street, and children who had been waiting with hand-carts pounced upon it with shrieks of delight.

'We have a strike on our hands,' Giovanni said. 'This island depends on sulphur. When we sell sulphur we eat, and when we don't we go hungry. Heard about Monterosso? They tied up the guards and dumped them into boiling sulphur. I was given this information by the engineer himself, an exquisite gentleman who always has gold-leaf stirred into his after-dinner brandy. Do you know what I'd do to the strikers?'

'Put them up against the wall,' I said. Like most waiters Giovanni viewed all such crises through the eyes of affluent customers.

'Exactly right,' he said. 'Just that. Shoot the lot. I'd have no mercy on them. But the trouble is there's nobody to do it. We have no army and no police. My son's a corporal in the carabinieri and in his section they have three pairs of boots between five men. The fact is we're at the mercy of the Reds.'

'So what's the solution?' I asked.

'We have to bring back the Allies. They should never have left us. It's our only hope.'

I spent the afternoon settling myself in the old office I had occupied during the last few months of the war, which by the greatest of good luck was still vacant. Palma suffered disastrous earthquakes roughly once in every generation, but minor tremors were a routine matter adding a spicing of excitement to life, particularly in the dull winter months. Occasionally a building gave up the ghost and fell in a heap somewhere in the town, but usually the inhabitants were dragged out alive. My office was in theory a condemned building on the edge of a fault, from which came faint creakings and whisperings, regularly audible simply by putting one's ear to the cracked pavement on the ground floor. The inspector at the Town Hall in charge of such matters, still a little stunned by one of the hangovers that commonly followed the march, came round to look the place over and I made him a small courtesy payment for his trouble and the provision of a key.

'So you're happy to take a chance?' he said, poking with his comb into one of the cracks in the wall.

'Why not? It looked much the same when I was last here.'

'It's hissing a bit now,' he said. 'That's just a phase. Keep your ears open for a noise like a cough. If you hear that, get out. It usually happens at two or three in the morning. I'd recommend sleeping under the bed rather than in it.'

Things were much as I had left them, although in the interim since my last tenancy most of the window-panes had gone, and the gaping frames had snatched many small flying creatures from the air; the husks of moths with huge, staring eyes in their wings, a long-dead bat, shoulders hunched like a cloaked assassin, tiny eyeless songbirds, their claws clenched in agony, translucent, crackling locusts, blown all the way from Africa. The old, awkward, army furniture was still in place, now coated with chalky dust in which some curious visitor had traced with a finger-tip pornographic drawings of outstanding artistic merit. Nothing worked – but then it hardly ever had – and I was amazed that after some hours of tinkering a little sherry-coloured water twisted from a tap, and the lamp filaments glowed feebly when the electricity was turned on. I investigated my rations, delivered by the last of our DRs in Sicily, confirming once more that the Army remained unable to work out an arrangement for supporting less than twelve men in the field and that in addition to twelve sets of instructions for combating VD, I had received a dozen packs of bacon and as many of sugar – both having inestimable trade value in this area of absolute dearth.

Included, too, with the rations was a notice *UFFICIO RECLAMI*, and the unnecessary translation beneath, CLAIMS OFFICE. This was in response to the Colonel's idea that I should present some official excuse for my presence in Palma. 'Otherwise they might ask awkward questions. Why not say you're running a claims office?' he suggested. 'I've discovered that this town was absolutely pillaged by our troops, and there are outstanding claims by the hundred.'

'Nobody will be taken in,' I objected. 'These people are not fools. This is another example of cover for cover's sake. It'll create a good deal of work besides drawing attention to me.' I nailed up the board, tacking over it a small typewritten note: 'Claimants seen on Mondays only, 10–12 a.m. Be brief.'

With the coming of evening preparations were at an end. Homeless dogs scenting human occupation from afar had begun to hang about the place, smiling hopefully, and a clairvoyant had left a handbill guaranteeing to inform me whether my wife was unfaithful to me, and if so with whom. I decided that it was too late now to call on my friends, and put off all visits until the morrow: to the Marchesina in her ruined palace, to my lawyer friend Avvocato Crispi, distinguished authority on feudal practices, to Dr Moscato who earned a pittance as curator of the museum.

This, although spring in Sicily, was by our standards munificent and flawless summer, perfumed with aromatic sap, at this hour with the heat of the day gone out of the straw-coloured sky. I locked up the office, then strolled down to the shore, cataloguing the contents of the street as I went: seven scampering young seminarians, skirts flying like Caucasian dancers. Second old rider on a white horse. Man grilling sparrows for sale. Man walking two lunatics on leads. Stork nesting on tower, rising to allow eggs to cool. Women washing over house with deep ochreous colour, 'to stop the sun from eating it'. Seller of nuts with poster, 'They will assist you to think' ... Then, by the shore, ballad singer celebrating new cult-hero Giuliano, 'I sing of a bandit in bed with a duchess.' Three painted fishing boats with cows' horns projecting from their prows. Finally the four ruined palaces of Palma, leaning on each other for support in the last stages of decrepitude, as they lurched towards the sea into which, sooner or later, they would inevitably fall. The last of these, the Prizzi Palace, was occupied by the Marchesina with whom I had conducted a fitful love affair since my first arrival in Sicily. We had a pact that in no circumstances would I ever pay a visit without previous warning so I scribbled a note and pushed it through the gate. '*Eccomi quà*. Calling tomorrow a.m. Love as ever, John.'

2

I CLANGED THE BELL and within moments the gate was opened
by the Marchesina's dog-faced and half-mad servant known
as the Seaweed Eater, who received me with a wrinkled nose
and the familiar, wall-eyed stare, thereafter backing away as
if in loathing. She walked off seeming to have dismissed me
and I followed her into the courtyard, finding, as I had
feared I would, resounding emptiness. 'Is your mistress at
home?' I asked, and she wrinkled her nose again. 'Hold your
horses. She's on her way down. She'd fly if she had wings.'
She ducked out of sight through a gothic arch, reminding
me of the entrance to a crypt. I heard the sound of a door
open above in the cabin the Marchesina had built for herself
on the gallery at the top of the monumental staircase after

the collapse of most of the back of the building, and in a moment she came into sight, waved to me, then came tripping down the stairs. I was afraid that she might be put out because I had given her no time to furnish the ground floor on a temporary basis with the throne-like chairs, the pictures, the tapestry, the pennants and the suit of armour shared equally between the four palaces. At least she had been able to dress for the occasion in the vaguely Grecian style she found suitable in these surroundings. She reached the bottom of the staircase and we fell into each other's arms. She was as beautiful as ever, and in my opinion at 43 the best-preserved woman in Sicily and possibly the world. There was not a trace of a wrinkle anywhere on her skin, her fair hair fell in a lustrous deluge on her shoulders, and the splendid eyes were as full as ever of vivacity and mirth. 'Welcome home,' she said. 'So you are here again as I knew you would be. *Chè bella sorpresa!* Did you come back to spy on us again?'

'I came back for you.'

'Of course you did,' she said, gently ironic. 'And how long will you be staying this time?'

'As long as I can. That I promise you. I was rock-climbing in Wales, neither really alive nor dead, and I heard there was something going on in Sicily, and I jumped at it.'

'Apart from me, where does the attraction lie?'

'It's an escape back into a kind of war.'

'And why should you want to do that?'

'Because war puts an end to the search for order which most of us find so uncomfortable. It's like joining a fatalistic religion — Islam, if you like — and throwing back the responsibility for your life into God's lap. I'm in this, you think to yourself, and there's nothing I can do about it, so why worry? From the first day in Sicily I fell in love with it.

You Sicilians are like the Arabs, although worse in most ways. You take no thought for the morrow, and that suited me.'

'This is Pirandello's chaos,' she said.

I agreed. 'I thrive on it,' I said.

'And you're back in your old office in the Via Pace, aren't you?'

'How did you guess?'

'It's inevitable. You like it because it will fall down one day.'

I laughed, although a little taken by surprise. There was probably some truth in this. 'Everything's possible,' I said. 'They offered me a room in a new building clear of the fault, but I was fond of the old place.'

'And you didn't marry after all.'

'I don't think I was ever really serious about it. It was something I felt I ought to do. Forty, I thought. It has to be now or never. Then I started to worry about the house, and all the furnishings and fittings, and the commitments and the circle of friends, and the mealtimes and the clocks, and about accepting the responsibilities of life, and I put it off.'

'Of course you did. Marriage is for neither of us. I am as free as the air.'

And this was true, but not entirely of her own choosing. Girls of noble but impoverished families unable to put up the cash for an appropriate marriage settlement frequently remained unmarried. A single opportunity of escape from this situation had occurred during the war when she had been courted by an American officer until permission to marry was refused following a secret report by the Italian police describing her as irretrievably promiscuous. Of this episode her only reference to me had been, 'I once had a narrow escape'.

Her skin seemed to glow in the medieval gloom as if lit from within by lamps. She presented her perfect left profile, the face of innocence like that of Benozzo Gozzoli's *Lucrezia*. The invisible temple on the right side featured a tiny brown mole that she had never been persuaded to have excised. There was the faintest possible whiff about her – or so I imagined – of sulphur dioxide, and I remembered the circle of enthusiasts to which she belonged who spent much time in fine weather running up and down the slopes of the volcano in search of newly opened fissures which released beneficial gases. She talked endlessly and with great vivacity on trivial subjects between the kisses. Currents far more powerful, more swirling and more complex than those that jostle the iron filings on a sheet flowed from her, and I responded with enthusiasm. I was fascinated by everything about her, by her great and delicate beauty despite her years, her almost frantic vitality, her absolute disdain for the opinion of the world around, also by her uniquely aristocratic Sicilian capacity for disbelief. Like most members of the great families that supplied the island's bishops and its archbishops, she was an atheist.

She said, 'Life here in your absence has been very dull. We play canasta, and because of the food situation we talk of hardly anything else, and those who get the chance make love. We have grand parties once a month, when we put all the furniture together and someone like the Cardinal's secretary agrees to come. There are certain fish caught here which the ordinary people despise because they don't understand how they should be cooked, but we do, and we can buy them from the fishermen very cheaply. In a way you come at a bad time because it is not my turn for the furniture until the week after next. Until then we sleep on the floor, stand up to talk, and even to copulate, and drink out of jugs.

13

When the furniture comes back we will have a big party, but you must bring your rations unless you want to eat cactus paste and beans. Here the food problem remains unchanged.'

I nodded sympathetically. The four patrician families were rich only in pretensions and memories. Like most of the great landlords of Sicily, they had passed their country estates over into the hands of a rapacious class of stewards and themselves retired to the cities, where they lived in dignified penury, growing mushrooms in their old wine cellars and rearing chickens in their banqueting halls. In Palma the last straw had been the town's occupation by prestigious English regiments, who had stripped the great houses and carried away everything of value: Bokhara carpets, Aubusson tapestries, Capodimonte crockery, Grecian vases and Roman busts, gold crosses wrenched from the necks of Amharic noblemen, old-master paintings, Etruscan statuary and Renaissance sculpture; plus – although unrealized as such by their owners – the greatest collection of fakes ever assembled.

We sat on a stone bench facing a fountain by Volpone, too heavy to be included among the loot. A sea-nymph stranded on the fountain pointed her breasts in our direction. Once she had squirted water from her nipples at the unwary visitor making a close approach for inspection – a familiar sixteenth-century joke – but now the pump, the water clocks and the trip-switches had long since broken down. There was no flow of water either, but a moment before the Seaweed Eater had sprinted past on her way to the ladder she would climb like a steeplejack to some remote attic where a number of filled pitchers stood beside a tank at the head of the system, ready to be emptied into it. In a moment water began to drip then drizzle from the naiad's breasts. A few spurts wetted the greenish patina of the stone belly, and for the moment the show was over. The Marchesina gurgled with pleasure. It was the little performance she prepared for all her visitors, but I had seen it many times before.

'Don't you think she's like me?' she asked as usual, referring to the naiad.

'I do,' I said, and she was.

'The model was an Aragonese girl of good family. We have similar features. The Allies couldn't take the fountain away but they broke her nose. The Seaweed Eater stuck it back. She's very practical.'

'Also very impolite. At least to me.'

'It's an instinctive dislike,' she said. 'Jealousy could come into it. We don't dare criticize her because we need her to shift the furniture about. She's as strong as an ox, besides which she knows where to find medicinal herbs on the volcano. If she weren't here we'd go without greenstuff; chicory and asparagus for example, and of course dandelions which are practically extinct, and money can't buy. There's no one to equal her when it comes to looking for snails. Without the Seaweed Eater I don't know where we'd be.'

'And what does she get out of this?'

'The association. She's accepted into noble houses almost as a member of the family. When she goes out with one of us to carry the shopping she's no longer expected to walk a few paces in the rear. I don't expect her to address any of my friends as Your Excellency. The fact is she used to be dependent upon us. Now we're dependent upon her. My friends even take her to church. It's enough of a reward to be seen with them.'

Having gone through her act with the fountain the Seaweed Eater reappeared. She had been barefoot until now, but at this point she put on a pair of shoes made from tyresoles and went slapping about the courtyard with a show of great activity, accompanied by blustering sighs. Firewood had been stacked in a far corner by a stove. In a moment blue smoke began to arise. She next slapped away through a gothic archway and I heard the sound of a pump being worked and the splash of water, and in a matter of seconds she returned with a cooking pot; this she put on the stove, then squatted in a position where she could keep us under watch.

'Doesn't she ever go away?' I asked.

'She's nowhere to go.'

'You mean she stays here watching you all the time?'

'Most of the time. She'll have to go out to collect the driftwood for the fire sooner or later, but she won't while you're here. Does she distract you? She doesn't me. It's just like having a dog about the place. I forget she's there.'

'Could we go upstairs?'

'Surely you know their mentality? There'd be a terrible scene. She'd probably run out into the street and make a spectacle of herself. In any case, you know the rules. I don't find these surroundings suitable for love-making.'

'I've a car outside. Can we go somewhere else?'

'I feel the same about this town as I do about the house.'

'Acireale, then?'

'I hate the place. Let's make it Marinella. On Thursday. Happy?'

'Yes, but it seems a long time to wait.'

'I have my good reasons for that,' she said.

3

Leaving the marchesina I called on my friend Dr Moscato in the museum where he had accepted the post of curator at a wage the equivalent of eighteen shillings a week. I had no reason to suppose he was not delighted to see me, but in the Sicilian manner he received me without surprise, rather as if we had parted company after discussing some unsatisfactory business only a few days before. 'How are things?' I asked. 'Why ask? You can see for yourself,' he said. His expression was irrevocably outraged. 'As our saying goes, *"O l'amicuzia o la soru bedda,"* meaning a friend in court, or a pretty sister, of which I possess neither.' He was a tactless man who had ruined his career by criticizing people it would have been safer to leave alone, including Mussolini for seducing every woman who ever came to see him, Marshal Badoglio for losing battles, and the Pope for his alleged possession of a gold telephone. As a result, having once been a consultant in urinology, he now presided over a unique collection of fossilized toads and several cases of pickled exhibits demonstrating the growth of the foetus in a horse. Just as in the Marchesina's case, his English was near-perfect.

I took out a packet containing about a quarter of a pound of bacon, and handed it to him. He opened it, peeled off a slice, and shook his head in wonderment. Although he was probably deeply grateful, custom prevented him from showing it.

He seemed about to put the slice in his mouth.

'It needs cooking,' I told him.

'Am I a fool?' he said.

He reached for a bottle on a shelf, poured a little colourless liquid into two measuring glasses, then added and stirred in a pinch of violet powder. He pushed one of the glasses towards me. 'It's fresh,' he said, 'delivered today. Won't do you any harm.' This I realized was preserving fluid for his specimens to which he had added gentian by way of flavouring. I took the glass, filled my mouth with precautionary saliva, sipped the spirit then turned away my head to conceal the wince as I swallowed.

'Like it?' Moscato asked. 'Pulls you together, doesn't it? I'm trying to think of anything that's happened while you've been away. Oh yes, we've had a miracle in the town. About a hundred and fifty women whose husbands have been overseas for up to three years in PoW camps have given birth – an unusually high proportion of twins, and in one case, black twins. Who've you seen so far?'

'The Marchesina.'

'Is that crazy maid still with her?'

'As ever.'

'She was in court while you were away for supplying aphrodisiacs, contrary to the Dangerous Drugs Act. The Marchesina appeared for her and they let her go.'

'Our old friend Crispi was involved this time,' he went on. 'On the receiving end. You remember a widow with six children who got her clutches on him? It came out that she'd bought some of the stuff and fed it to him.'

'Surely he'd be too starved for it to have much effect.'

'A mild degree of starvation doesn't count for much in that direction. It hasn't done the widow any good. He's fallen for a fifteen-year-old girl and intends to marry her. You'll be seeing him. You have to help me convince him he's out of his mind. By the way, what are you doing here? No fables please.'

'I'm asking a few questions.'

'What about?'

'The separatists.'

'I guessed it would be that. Did you go on the March?'

'I didn't actually take part, no.'

'You would have learned something to astonish you. Great decisions were taken. You would have witnessed the spectacle of a people united in resolve.'

'Can you say any more about it?'

'At this stage no. The town expects some sort of public declaration tonight.'

'Of support for separatism?'

'You must wait for the announcement, but let's say I shouldn't be surprised. I may as well admit that I see the separatists as our salvation. My private and personal view is that we're the victims of a conspiracy designed to put an end to our Christian civilization.'

19

'I thought you didn't believe in God, Doctor.'

'I'm not talking about legends invented to keep women and children quiet. This is a way of life. No one denies that foreign agents have been infiltrated into the country. How else do you account for the fact that thirty-six thousand miners are on strike and the peasants are refusing to till the soil? As I see it only the separatists with the Allies at their back can throw back the Red tide.'

'Apart from that how do you feel about them?'

'I've never attempted to conceal my allegiance. This island is no better than an Italian colony. You know what the Italians say – "Africa begins south of Rome". They treat us like blacks. Look at me. I'm a typical victim of Italian neo-colonialism which has reduced me to penury.'

He pressed down on his desk top with his big, bony hands to lever himself with a faint creaking of joints to his feet, a tall cadaverous man, martyred by indignation. 'Why are the northern universities open when Catania's closed?' he asked. 'I could have been lecturing in the medical school at Catania.' He went to a cupboard and came back laden with the museum's three prize exhibits – the cadavers of a mother, father and child, the victims it was said of sinister nineteenth-century experimentation which had digested the muscular tissue leaving nothing but blood vessels and bones. He shook them urgently and they rustled like autumn leaves caught up by the wind, and the sunshine shafting through his window filled with motes. 'They pay me five hundred lire a week to give a talk on this rubbish,' he said. I had tried in the past to get Moscato to admit that these exhibits were fakes, but he refused. 'The Prince made a contract with his servants. He gave them a sum of money and a year to spend it in, and after that he experimented on them with the result that you see. The trouble is the public has got tired of them. They've lost their appeal. They don't work for us any more.'

He bundled the corpses back into the cupboard and fell into his chair. 'Give Crispi my regards,' he said. 'Ask him to take you down to the Square tonight if he's free. They're staging what they call an act of spontaneous support for the cause and handing out flags. You might bring me one back.'

I went to pick Crispi up at his lodgings at the end of a dark alleyway where I found him at work on a large and fanciful genealogical chart tacked on a wall. The small house was full of young children and everything that went with them; screamings and bawlings, toys to be tripped over, infantile smells, splashes on floors. At one moment in an interlude of scolding a door flung open, and a large, dishevelled and very pregnant woman stood there to scan us with injured eyes before withdrawing. 'How long, O Lord? How long?' Crispi groaned. He let go my hand and jumped to his feet. 'Let's go out somewhere and celebrate,' he said.

Crispi had practised for twenty years in the Italian north, and the experience had cured him of any Sicilian reserve from which he might have suffered. He was jolly and expansive, and semi-starvation, which treats people in different ways, had in his case produced an unconvincing inflation. He bounced along at my side, stopping from time to time to take breath, and uttering cries of astonishment and delight at my unexpected return. 'Such a relief to see you. I'm sorry you found me when you did. It's been a martyrdom, but the end's in sight. Half our sub-post-office fell down the other day and the staff refuse to work there any longer, so I may be able to move in. Another thing, at the post-office I'll be able to work on bigger charts. As you know, all these people who did well out of the black market are looking round for ancestors. Where I am now there's not enough wall-space to go back to the Aragonese, and all the people who really cleaned up want Angevins, which puts on another three or four feet in height.'

'Why the Angevins?'

'If you've read your history, you'll remember they raped all the women. You've heard of the Sicilian Vespers. That means they had bigger balls – or so my clients suppose. They're the kind of ancestors any real man wants to have, and I'm the one who can supply them. Where shall we go?'

'Moscato said something might be happening in the Square.'

'That's right, the flag distribution. Let's go down there. How was he, by the way?'

'In great form.'

'Did he say anything about his troubles?'

'No.'

'He had a gangster friend. You wouldn't know about that. They went to school together. Prefect Mari had him banished to Milan at the time of the purge, but they've always kept in touch. This friend of his has got himself mixed up with the Reds in his old age. He's sending down some trouble-maker and wants Moscato to look after him. Moscato of all people. He's just as much of a fascist as he always was. Moscato can't stop worrying about it. He can't face the idea of letting his friend down. Pity he couldn't have come along tonight.'

It was early evening again, the time in a hot country when the day really comes into its own, and people go out to draw the cool air into their lungs, and find somewhere with greenery – even a single tree – in sight, to talk and to think about

22

very little and make the most of an enclave of peace in their existence. The Square when we got there reminded me as it always did of a theatre of the old kind, with a stage in the middle of the audience. The citizens of Palma who had come here had sorted themselves into categories and groups based upon intricate standards of prestige and acceptance in which birth, wealth, education, profession, political outlook, but above all *the power to persuade others* played a part. Three clubs, in ascending order of dignity, the Association of ex-Combatants, the Cultural Circle and the Civilized People's Club, were ranged on the east side under the background of the volcano, the members in each case placed in silent motionless rows, resembling Easter Island figures, as they watched through the clubs' plate-glass windows the area where the stage should have been. Across the Square the generality of the population had taken their usual places outside cafés and bars. Here, too, there was little movement, and no more than a respectful scraping of chairs in the way of noise. When we arrived late-comers were trickling in ones and twos into view, making for the seats they always occupied, and I knew that in a matter of minutes every one would be taken. There was not a woman to be seen.

Crispi and I took our seats outside the Roma at a table kept for him by an understanding with the aged head-waiter who received free legal advice, whenever required, in return. We sat there for some time and nothing happened, nothing was expected to – this was part of the ritual, Crispi had previously explained; and then at about seven p.m., with the sun well above the horizon, by the old Arab reckoning the twelve hours allotted to the day were at an end, and officially it was night. This was confirmed by a single, powerful clank of the bell of the Church of St Maria della Vittoria, thrusting its pinnacled shadow half across the

Square, and instantly – and it was only to be supposed that he had been waiting under cover for the signal – the police marshal in his long purple cloak made his entrance on his way to the Cultural Circle, and with this the waiters came scurrying into view with their steaming jugs. Overhead, accurately timed for this curtain-raising, and perfectly spaced in the yellowing sky, a procession of storks trailed themselves nestwards. I counted fourteen in all, a magic number by local credence.

'When does the spontaneous demonstration happen?' I asked Crispi.

'Any moment now,' he said.

As he spoke an aged car, its snouted front pressed to the earth, came snuffling down a narrow street facing us into the Square, and I realized that Minasola, our man of respect, who normally preferred the rural scene, was paying the town one of his infrequent visits. Every head was raised or turned as the car rattled round the square to come to a standstill outside the Civilized People's Club. The driver and the passenger, both of them countrymen in breeches and gaitered boots, got out and went in, and all the members who had been seated facing the square rose to their feet together. They then resumed their seats.

'Did you notice anything?' Crispi asked.

'Is there anything I should have?'

'The flag,' he said. 'The yellow flag on Minasola's car.'

'And what does that signify?'

'It signifies his decision to join the movement.'

'And if he joins it, everybody does.'

'I quite understand this is inexplicable to you,' Crispi said. 'Let's put it like this, they'll be considerably influenced.'

'Can you explain why?'

'It would be impossible to explain. It would take too long, I'm not sure that we know ourselves.'

'Are all these people pleased?'

'Most of them are overjoyed.'

'But showing it in the usual way.'

'You should know us by now.'

'I'm still waiting for the spontaneous support,' I said.

'Do you expect them to clap, or cheer? Look for yourself. Just take a look round. It's happened.'

The three taciturn men at the next table were drinking amarettos, suggesting a celebration, with their coffees. I noticed little yellow flags in their lapels. Some wore stars as well in indication of their desire, Crispi said, for Sicily to become an American State. The men at the table beyond them wore yellow flags also. I turned back to Crispi, noting that he too had been ready with his flag and was in the act of pinning it in position. I laughed. 'Influenced, I see.'

'It wasn't necessary in my case,' he said.

'I didn't notice anybody handing the flags out.'

'Most people brought them with them.'

'I believe Moscato would like one if there happens to be a spare one going.'

Crispi patted his pocket. 'I have it here.'

There was a movement of Easter Island figures in the Civilized People's Club across the Square. All the members in the window seats got up, then sat down again. 'Minasola's going,' Crispi said. 'He never wants to stay more than a few minutes.'

The man of respect and his driver came shuffling down the steps of the club, got into the vintage Renault and went rattling away.

With that a change in the atmosphere was noticeable.

25

Men at the neighbouring tables began to talk in a more animated way. Some of them got up, strolled a few paces and sat down again. There was an air almost of relief, as if the withdrawal of a royal personage now permitted some relaxation in small matters of social protocol. There seemed fewer yellow flags in evidence.

Crispi said he had a chart to finish and I walked back with him part of the way to his lodgings. It was still quite light, but the sun was setting somewhere out of sight, the sky had turned to gun metal, and banks of shadow slid from the tall buildings into the street. The small bars in the vicinity were crowded with men playing the noisy and aggressive card-game scopa with the sound of rooks congregating at their nesting sites. An official dog-catcher carrying what appeared to be a huge butterfly net hurried past on his rounds in search of potentially dangerous strays.

'Forgive me,' Crispi said, 'but I feel the need to talk to someone. No doubt Moscato told you about the widow. Have you heard of the species of wasp that captures a caterpillar, paralyses it with its sting, and then keeps it as a source of fresh food to be fed upon at leisure? That's been my situation.'

'Surely you're exaggerating, Avvocato?'

'Not at all. I've been a prisoner, virtually deprived of my will power, unable to escape.'

'How can such a thing happen?'

'I can't tell you in so many words. We're dealing with a clever woman. Pressure can be exerted in all sorts of subtle ways. A slow process. I could practically feel myself being tied up. What I wanted to say is, you've arrived at a particularly happy moment. I've been saved by the love of a beautiful girl. I'm just about to tear myself free.'

'Which won't be particularly easy, or pleasant, I imagine.'

'No,' he said. 'But it's now or never. I feel I've got something to live for and it's given me strength.'

'When's the happy event been fixed for, Avvocato?'

'We haven't got as far as that. First comes the contract. Naturally you and Moscato are invited to the signing.'

'I'm most honoured. And warmest congratulations,' I said. 'I'm very happy for you.'

Crispi stopped for breath, and spotting a defaced stone lion that protruded from the wall nearby he rested for a moment on its head, then jumped to his feet smiling and we moved on. How resilient humans could be, I thought. How little, when it came to the point, they required not only to exist but to breed optimism and hope. Crispi at the age of 55, and entangled with a vigorous, demanding and possibly even vengeful harridan, could still reach out for love.

We were nearing the corner of the fetid lane in which he lived. He slowed down. 'To some extent,' he said, 'my situation's been helped by good news in other directions. The party is finding me a steady job.'

'The party?'

He tapped the flag in his lapel. 'The movement. It's on the cards I'll be made legal adviser for the province.'

'Why that's tremendous news. When's this to happen?'

'As soon as they take over. This month. Next month. Things are moving very fast. You saw how it was today.'

'From our conversations in the past I never thought of you as a separatist, Avvocato.'

'And you were right. Why should I attempt to pull the wool over your eyes? My enthusiasm for the movement is not wholly disinterested. In the politics of our country everyone looks for a reward.'

4

Days of fact-finding followed in preparation for a report. Professional men such as Dr Moscato and Avvocato Crispi provided the solid material, but there were many other less substantial sources of information not wholly to be disdained.

There was the Archpriest, who believed that God was a mathematician, and ran a bank as a sideline, and a multitude of supernumerary priests whose sparse religious activities left them with much time on their hands and a proclivity for gossip, who were by no means shy of drawing upon a stock in trade of confessional secrets if there seemed to be a demand for them. They headed the category of people in close contact with others, confidants of both sexes and all classes, and if it was a matter of gauging the drift of public opinion there were few to equal them. Next in line came prostitutes – the so-called Englishwomen – in their painted caravans on the roads leading into the town. A high percentage of males visited these dignified and knowledgeable women at one time or another, and most of them ran a sideline in clairvoyance and crystal-gazing for women customers. The problem here was their huge contempt for men who went in for sexual time-wasting, but this could be got round by gifts of streaky bacon and palm-reading sessions.

Inevitably I talked to the police, as little daunted as possible by the complications arising from the existence of two competitive and mutually hostile forces, the Carabinieri and the Pubblica Sicurezza, each determined to refute the other's point of view, and damage each other in any way they could. My excuse was the claims-file which I took along for their supposed advice, but they invariably laughed it aside and we got down to the serious business of the day. I went from station to station feeding policemen with bacon and doing my best to keep up their spirits with wholly unrealistic forecasts of better times to come. Old Giovanni of the Roma had given me a note for his carabiniere son and it proved to be no exaggeration when he claimed that the five men of his post possessed only six boots between them, obliging two members of the squad to go on patrol in tyre-soled shoes. The carabinieri here shared two World War I Mauser rifles and a handful of cartridges from that period, most of them considered defective. They had reason to congratulate themselves that Salvatore Giuliano, claimed by the press to be the most formidable bandit in the history of a country glutted with banditry, was still fully occupied in the mountains some one hundred miles away, and they were greatly dismayed by the generally accepted story that he had been named commander of the armed forces of the separatists mustering in the far west. Above all they were demoralized and embittered by the knowledge that while ordinary policemen were being slaughtered by the bandits, the generals and colonels in command of one police force and the chief inspectors of the other should have held the most cordial meetings and even banqueted with the bandit-in-chief. In this way they, too, had demonstrated their separatist sympathies.

The report would be a concoction of a special kind for the eyes of higher echelons of the service, with clear-cut edges, eschewing subtleties and doubt, presenting a façade of apparently unvarnished truth, yet on closer examination a species of fiction. Rank and power increasingly distanced those at the top from the complexities of reality. But since the Colonel as yet had only one foot across the crystal threshold of illusion it was still possible to sway him to the belief that in this situation the wind constantly changed direction, that Sicilian politics were a secret art, that here a man could serve two masters, and that nothing was ever as it seemed.

I wrote him a separate, rather rambling letter on the subject. 'This is a pocket of feudalism hardly changed for a thousand years in a country tottering after the impact of war. Where there was one political party, now there are more than thirty — all at each others' throats. The word democracy is in everyone's mouth, but nobody has the faintest idea what it is all about. There's a brisk sale for religious ikons depicting the bandit Giuliano, regarded by many villagers as a saint. The real rulers, the landowners and princes of the Church, are there as before, and they have the power of medieval kings. We have a duke who owns seven palaces, each with several hundred rooms, and can still imprison his enemies in his own dungeons. The law forbids the employment of children under ten years of age in the sulphur mines, but the companies laugh at it. A few days ago they held what is called the March of the Long Shadows in this town. It's something they've probably been doing for thousands of years. When it was over they all decided they were going to be separatists. But you can never tell. Something can happen to make them change their minds overnight. If the Italian State ever succeeds in pulling itself to its feet again, it'll put an end to all this kind of thing, and they know it. Feudalism can't go on for ever. Naturally enough they want to cut adrift. Therefore they hope for our support. Either ours or the Americans – or both.'

By chance the report and the letter were picked up three days earlier than expected by the lone DR who found himself obliged to bump back on his Norton over the terrible roads to deliver a letter the Colonel had sent by extraordinary priority. This dealt more with ESP than Sicily.

The presence of the Colonel and me in Baghdad had had little, in my opinion, to do with the war effort but more with the Colonel's current interest in archaeological sites. I was beginning to suspect that our watching brief in Sicily might be in some way bound up with his fascination for a country he had never visited and a monograph he had written on its Bourbon monarchy. Much of it, he admitted, had been devoted to the singular personality of Ferdinand IV. Contemporary accounts supplied by the municipality of Palermo had convinced him that the King was the archetypal benevolent despot. 'Everybody adored him,' the Colonel said. 'Strangely enough he ate very little but spaghetti. Not only did his skin exude the odour of sanctity but was said to possess a sweet savour. Favoured courtiers were sometimes rewarded by being allowed to lick an inch or two of his forearm. He was the first of the separatists.'

The next day I was in the office filling in a small crack that had suddenly appeared in the wall when the phone, normally dead, surprisingly tinkled, and when I picked it up the Colonel was on the line from London. This astonished me because it meant they must have sent out a coded message from Palermo as soon as the DR got in. I was also surprised because the use of a telephone was normally debarred, although such precautions often went by the board when only fairly routine matters were under discussion.

'Thanks for the communications,' he said. 'Fascinating. Quite an eye opener. Bit of a minefield for you, I should say. That thing about the march sounds astonishing. The sudden display of stars could be a straw in the wind. Any views on the subject?'

'I think opinion is beginning to veer in that direction.'

It was an exceedingly good connection, and listening to his voice I could almost see the slight change in his facial expression. 'I'm surprised in a way. I should have thought we were quite a good bet.' I sensed that he felt that I was lukewarm, and that his nationalistic hopes had not been entirely abandoned.

'The ruling classes are very pro-British,' I said. 'Most of them had Scotch nannies.'

'And of course went to one or other of our public schools,' he said.

'It could swing back,' I said. 'In a way these people remind me of termites. One is tempted to see them as operating through a group mind.'

He jumped in eagerly. 'A disembodied super-organism. How very interesting. It's an extraordinary thought. I was intrigued by your piece of information that they're making a saint of Giuliano. There was something about him in the *Times* the other day. Actually I was ringing to know if you have any contact with him.'

'None at all, but he's by no means difficult to contact.'

'I ask because two young friends of ours, American journalists, are trying to get in touch with him. They're after what used to be called a scoop. I know you'd like them. Anything you can do?'

'I don't know, but I can try.'

'Be most grateful if you would. Our Ambassador in Rome would like us to do whatever we can. I'm ringing you because time's rather short. I gather they're in Sicily already and on their way down there, so you can expect them at any time. Be most grateful for anything you can do.'

It was about one o'clock, and I had hardly put down the phone when suddenly there was a great roaring of a car exhaust in the street below, and I looked down to see a large desert-camouflaged military vehicle blocking the way, with two or three dogs that had sprinted in from different directions to piss on its wheels. A man and a woman got out, the man in the kind of jungle fatigues still worn by pressmen nostalgic for warlike action and the woman in a long, strawberry-coloured flowered dress. I pushed open my window with some difficulty, and the man looked up and waved. He had a smiling cherubic face, shiny with sunburn. 'Hi, John,' he said. 'We just came over from Palermo. A friend of yours told us to look you up. Rod Stein of the *Tribune*. Can we come up?'

I went down to unbolt the door. Rod proved to be quite bald under the floppy hat he wore, although no older, I would have said, than in his late twenties. Every part of his body was on the move, shaking like a blancmange with energy, and he kept up a continuous chuckle. The girl had a Mexican wetback face, with flat, placid eyes and jet black hair, and a sweet expression. Rod dropped a proprietorial hand on her shoulder. 'This is my wife,' he said, 'Nancy. She takes the pictures. I guess you've seen her shots in *Life*. We're on an assignment down here.'

'I heard that,' I said. 'Come on up.'

Rod glanced at a watch with an enormous, complicated face. 'Listen, John, I'm hungry. You free for lunch? Anywhere you know in town we could settle for a quiet chat over a plateful of pasta and a jug of wine?' He squeezed a brief but exuberant laugh between each sentence. 'How about you, Nancy? Ready for a mouthful of spaghetti?'

Nancy smiled thoughtfully and said in her soft, rich voice, she was.

I took them to the town's only restaurant, an austere room at the back of the Roma, with its splintered tables, its normally blocked lavatory, and its meek procession of beggars. A few black-hatted customers waiting for their food to be ready played scopa, greeting each win or loss with loud outcries of triumph or frustration. We were buzzed by enormous flies of several colours who had taken refuge indoors to escape the high wind of that morning which had now subsided.

Stein had seemed worried about leaving the car, and took it as a good joke when I assured him that apart from fairly frequent homicides, Palma di Cava was virtually free from crime. To settle his nerves I found a boy to make a pretence of guarding it.

He looked round for a menu. 'Do they have any speciality in a place like this?' Rod asked.

'No,' I told him. 'The food here is purely for survival. Minestrone, so-called, is the standby.'

'Do you think they might be able to do better than that?'

'Possibly,' I said, 'but let me explain the situation. Anything you and I would describe as food is in short supply and we're still in a barter situation. I draw army rations, largely bacon, much of which I use to buy friendship. The rest I bank here. They do whatever they want with it, and feed me with anything that happens to be going. This can be an adventure. Did they tell you in Palermo to bring something with you?'

'We brought cans of meat over from the States, but they suggested sugar, and we have that, too. We have about twenty kilos.'

'With twenty kilos of sugar you could practically buy the town,' I said. 'What had you in mind?'

'Pasta,' Stein said. 'But lots of it. Followed by meat. Whatever they happen to have. How does that sound to you, Nancy?'

'Just fine,' Nancy said. 'Really great.' It was wonderful what warmth, what feeling, what involvement she could inject into four words in her soft snuffling Chihuahua accent.

I took an immediate liking to her. 'There's just one thing I ought to mention. All the meat here is horse. It's bleached in a weak solution of chlorine and done up to look like veal. The alternative, called poultry, is city pigeon netted on the roofs.'

'Which do you personally recommend?' Stein asked.

'The horse.'

'The horse then let it be.'

'It's all part of the adventure,' Nancy said.

'That's the only way to look at it. Would it be easy to get out that sugar and excite them by letting them see it?' I asked Stein.

'Nothing could be easier.' He got up and went out to the car, and came back carrying the sugar in a US Forces pack. Our presence had already aroused interest among the hotel staff, causing the old waiter Giovanni to replace the striped pyjama top he normally donned to serve guests with a tail coat smirched with ancient stains. He hurried over at my signal. Sugar had been currency in the first year of the occupation, and everything once purchased with gold had been bought with it, until in the end we had appointed a powerful ex-criminal mayor of the town and he had helped put an end to the practice.

'Open it up for him,' I told Stein, and Stein broke open the top of the cardboard container. 'Sugar,' I said to the old man. 'Refined?' he wanted to know. 'Refined. The best.' The four scopa players at the next table watched us slyly over their cards like thieves alerted by the clink of coins.

'Give him a kilo,' I said to Stein, and to Giovanni, 'Bring us some good food.'

'I understand from the Colonel you're an old hand in these parts,' Stein said.

'In all I've been here for about two years. Most of it in the Army, then just recently again as a civilian settling up some old Army business. I'm on my own.'

'Don't you ever get tired of your own company?' Nancy asked.

'Frequently, but I've made a number of friends,' I said.

'Well, that's very nice. Local folk you mean?'

'Of all descriptions,' I told him. 'I find them quite interesting.'

'I imagine it's difficult to form rewarding friendships with members of the opposite sex?' Stein asked, his ready, good-natured grin reshaped by innuendo.

'Difficult, but not impossible.'

'They tell me Sicilian women age very quickly.'

Was it reasonable to use the Marchesina's indomitable resistance to the years, her enduring vigour and her zest, to defeat this commonplace? 'It's not true,' I assured him. 'On the contrary, many succeed in carrying their great beauty into old age. This is a country where one has to be on one's guard against stereotypes, because nothing will ever turn out to fit a preconception.'

'Thank you for putting me right, John,' Stein said, in instant and graceful retreat. 'Anyway, I gather you're happy to be here?'

'Let's say this, at this moment I can't think of any place where I'd prefer to be.'

The pasta came made with local greyish wheat, with its earthy flavour not wholly suppressed by fiery chillies. It was followed by horse stew, a lucky dip largely of offal in a murky tide of sauce. Stein ate like a man in a station restaurant with his eyes on his train due to leave within minutes. Nancy, too, demolished two large platefuls – eating daintily but with remarkable speed. Occasionally a distant rattle reached me from one or other stomach. Stein wiped his mouth with his handkerchief. 'Nancy and I do our best to eat well,' he said. 'Part of our philosophy of living. You know that stuff wasn't too bad?' He produced two enormous black pills, and he and Nancy with some difficulty swallowed one apiece. 'They contain *all* the minerals,' he said, and I detected triumph in his voice. Pausing for breath he asked questions that required no reply, and bombarded me with snippets of information. 'Maybe you agree with me, Sicily's a one-off place. They tell me you could buy a dukedom for ten thousand dollars up to a few years ago. How about all those painted carts you see about the place? Aren't they something? Is it a fact the women don't wear pants?'

Nancy forked a pouch-like object off her plate for closer examination.

'Somebody dropped a purse in this,' she said.

'That isn't a purse, it's a gland,' I said. 'I often come across them. I used to know it's name, but I've forgotten.'

She began a deft dissection. 'Well, I guess waste not want not,' she said.

Stein said, 'We plan to investigate Etna. Well, maybe not now, but later. Could you fill me in with the depth of the crater? I'm referring to the one subsequent to the nineteen-eleven eruption, but while you're about it it might be interesting to know just how deep the Monte Umberto crater is too, if that's still open. The nuns in the Ursuline Convent in Palermo sell cakes in the shape of women's breasts. I read somewhere you can buy donkey's meat for human consumption in any of these towns, and I can believe that, too. Excuse me, I'm just going out to make sure that guy I'm paying to watch the car hasn't fallen asleep.'

He came back carrying by the neck another bottle of wine he had picked up at the bar, and filled up our glasses. It was the strong, coarse, local stuff, black as ink, and not even filtered, from vines grown on laterite clay with too much exposure to the sun. When the glasses were held up to the light they showed hundreds of tiny particles held in suspension. Stein and Nancy drank without criticism. Stein said. 'This country's in a state of turmoil. They sure keep us news-hawks on the move. We were up at Bologna a couple of weeks ago. You may not have heard this, but the Reds were planning a takeover. They had parachute troops standing by in France ready to fly in and put it down. The newspaper paid a million dollars to a fixer for an exclusive on the start of the revolution. We actually told them where it had to happen. Imagine that. I even sold the film rights in advance, and hired myself a couple of movie cameramen.' He spread his large, soft, pliable hands in a gesture of anguish.

'So what happened?'

'An arms shipment was coming down from across the border back of Trieste. We paid out one hundred thousand dollars for the frontier guards to be included in the fix, but something went wrong and they were left out. The thing died on us. A piece of terrible luck.'

'What are you doing down here?'

'I imagine it's what you'd suppose, John. Sniffing out trouble. We were back in Washington last week, and someone said Bologna was a straw in the wind. They have an Italian office in the State Department, and the guy who saw me said the whole country could go Red. You won't believe me, but this guy's first name was Aesculapius. Anyway, I guess I'm ready to take his word for it. I don't have any personal views on the matter. Wars and rumours of wars, John.' There was a burst of apologetic laughter. 'I guess it's all in our line of business.'

Giovanni cleared away the remains of the stew, and brought ricotta, which for me had no discernible taste, and late-crop Palma oranges which I regarded as the finest in the world. Even the act of peeling them (which Rod and Nancy accomplished with enormous speed and dexterity) released a mixture of sweet scents drawn from the earth, and Rod and Nancy ate two apiece. 'Can you find oranges like that elsewhere in Sicily?' Rod asked, and I told him you could not, and that the trees grew on ancient lava, and he and Nancy agreed that they would have to buy a crate or two to fly back to their friends at home.

Rod said, 'I spoke on the phone to your friend John Simmons, and I believe he's been twisting your arm on our behalf. He must have told you we were going to be down here chasing a scoop. We had a strong tip back in the States that Salvatore Giuliano will be named as commander of a separatist army in process of formation. The Colonel said that with your connections you might be able to fix up an interview for us with him.'

'It could probably be arranged,' I said. 'His headquarters are up in the mountains about a hundred miles from here. You realize he's still technically a bandit, but I don't envisage much of a problem in seeing him. The police prefer to keep out of his way. A local photographer went up there a few weeks ago and got some nice out-of-focus pictures of Giuliano and his mother. He had a picnic with them and came back full of admiration and joy.'

Nancy said, 'It's wonderful that the Sicilian people have thrown up a leader at last.'

'It's only a year or so since he was killing policemen,' I said.

'Could that have been part of the struggle against the residue of fascism?' Nancy wanted to know. Her expression had become soft, indulgent and motherly. She and Rod were to be numbered with the Colonel among the world's believers, I decided. They wanted to love their fellow men. 'I don't think this had much to do with fascism,' I told her. 'On the whole bandits stay out of politics.'

'Maybe we have a short memory,' Nancy said, 'but we don't seem to hear much of his past. He has a considerable following in the States. It's been our privilege to read copies of letters he's sent to our president. They show a remarkable grasp of world affairs. Both Rod and I were impressed by their evident sincerity.'

'My guess is he's going straight to the top,' Rod said. 'I took a ten-day crash course in Italian history before coming over here and what I learned convinces me that the Sicilians have been fed shit by the Duce and all the generals and politicians for the past twenty years, and now they feel the time has come to be led by a man of the people, a Sicilian of their own kind.'

I left them to their illusions – or what seemed illusions to me. What was the point in mentioning that Giuliano, author of persuasive letters sent, in addition to the American president, to Stalin, Winston Churchill, Einstein, Albert Schweizer and the Pope, was an illiterate, who had never set foot inside a school? To me it came as a welcome surprise that the hard-bitten profession followed by my two charming friends should in no way have diminished their basic capacity for enthusiasm and faith – even allowing for Rod's occasional cynicism, as evidenced in the case of the Bologna fix – and I found myself refreshed by this brief respite from the eternal scepticism of the people among whom I now lived.

Suddenly remembering the cutting from the previous week's *Corriere* I had forgotten to file, I took it out of my pocket and passed it to them. It was an account of the photographer's visit to the mountains, and I had already noticed a kind of reverence about the choice of words, and the manufactured wonderment usually employed in the reporting of religious occasions. Giuliano had put on a clean, white open-necked shirt to be photographed, and the photographer had taken a typical happy holiday shot, spontaneous and revealing, even if slightly blurred, of a hugely likeable young man, brandishing a bottle of wine, and his splendid matriarch of a mother in peasant dress. Either the camera had lied with the most polished skill, or there was a trace of nobility to be discovered in these faces. Who would not have trusted the laughing mother with all their possessions? Who would run from her son?

'There's your man,' I said.

Nancy shook her head in wonderment. 'This,' she said, 'is a good man.'

'And you really think he might agree to see us?' Rod asked.

'I'm pretty sure he would. Giuliano's not the man to duck publicity.'

'Would he be in hiding and somewhere in a cave?'

'No,' I said. 'From the last report he's back in his home village, in the house where he was born.'

'But if the law's on his tail, how can that happen?' Rod asked.

'He's the boss up there. It's his own little kingdom. The King of Montelepre. He has a plan for the redemption of the world, based on giving every marriageable girl a dowry of five-thousand lire. He's handed out a hundred or so dowries already.'

'Where does the money come from?'

'He used to hold up banks.'

'This is crazy,' Rod said.

'Here you're in Alice's Wonderland. Everything's turned upside down. You mustn't be surprised at anything. The police chief's a robber, the Archpriest runs the bank, and a bandit raises funds for the poor. It's the local brand of normality.'

'Sounds like this could be an even bigger story than I thought.'

'I might be able to arrange to take you up there, if you feel that would be of help,' I said.

Rod laid a restraining hand on my arm. 'John,' he said, 'that's a fantastic offer, and I certainly appreciate it. Nancy and I came down here because we figured it would be helpful to have your advice on this project. The last thing we would expect you to do would be to put yourself to that kind of trouble.'

'No trouble,' I said. 'For me it would be an excuse to get away. Every couple of weeks or so I make a point of taking off for the mountains for a change of scene. I take my old EMC up there and record the folk music if there's any to be found I'd enjoy coming with you if I wouldn't be in the way.'

'Well, in that case – ' Rod said, and Nancy put on her wide, tribal smile, and said it would be wonderful.

'There are certain preliminaries,' I said, 'which would take a day to arrange. The visit has to be cleared through our local man of respect.'

'The man of respect?'

'That's the way these things are done here. If we took off and went by ourselves, we'd run up against a blank wall. The man of respect will give us his blessing and there won't be any unforeseen hitches. He's an ex-goatherd called Minasola. He's no longer into goats but he keeps a thousand or so of them as pets. He's by way of being a close friend of the Cardinal's, and three or four of the more powerful princes. If he likes you he's always ready to help.'

'It looks like there's another story there,' Rod said.

'I would have thought that, too. It's an unusual system,' I said. 'There's no reason I can see why you shouldn't do a piece about it, mentioning no names.'

'John, I have to say this sounds a very exciting project. When do you imagine we might be able to take off?'

'It all depends how long it takes me to see Minasola. We could think in terms of the day after tomorrow. All these roads are bad, so it would mean an early start.'

There it was left and Rod and Nancy booked in for the night in the flea-bitten hotel. The Roma possessed a single dormitory into which were shifted as many beds as the

43

night's trade in travellers made necessary, privacy being provided by Japanese-style moveable partitions and screens. It was airless, plagued by mosquitoes that lived in the hotel's potted palms, and had access to sanitary arrangements of a daunting kind. These conditions were confronted with stoicism by my American friends. The only thing that seemed to worry them in any way was what to do with their enormous car. 'I just paid twenty-thousand bucks for it,' Rod said. They had filled the back with souvenirs, including a dismantled painted cart to take back to the US, and although the windowless body was padlocked they still seemed unhappy until a boy from the hotel agreed to sleep in the cabin.

At this point we parted company. Rod said that given the opportunity he and Nancy liked to go and 'bounce around for a while' after a good lunch, and it was arranged that we should meet again next day.

Next morning I went to see Minasola. I'd met him before when he was surrounded as usual by toadies who hung around him as if absorbing something of the mysterious influences he was supposed to exude, and no more than polite words had been exchanged. If you were not afraid of this man there was no difficulty about seeing him, and not only that, he was notoriously accessible to supplicants at any hour of the day or night, willing and apparently even eager to help them in any predicament they might be in. Everyone knew that he had been one of the three men of respect who had seen the Commander of the German troops in Western Sicily, the day after the Allied invasion, and persuaded him to withdraw without resistance, after guaranteeing his safety, and that of his soldiers. Minasola was a man of the purest, unsullied illiteracy, with fine animal intuitions and instincts never blunted by so much as an hour's formal education, and sharing a view of the world with the Archpriest, only reached by the latter after long years devoted to a study of divinity and the related sciences.

I found him outside his farmhouse feeding his pet owls with newly born mice. Owls were a common pet in Sicily, and Minasola, who was fond of animals and birds of all kinds, kept six of them on platforms fixed to posts in his yard, to which they were fastened by the legs by leather jesses. He greeted me in a friendly way, asked to be excused for a moment and went on with the feeding. Hanging from one post was a basket from which he picked the baby mice one by one, and when about to feed a bird it clearly amused him to try to take it by surprise by dodging behind it. This would cause the owl, without shifting its position on the perch, to swivel its head until it faced backwards, before taking the squirming mouse in a delicate, premeditated fashion in its beak, and the shallow, brilliant eyes of the bird that could detect the movement of a fly opening and closing its wings in the grass a hundred feet below, met the rheumy, bloodshot eye of the old man who clearly had some difficulty in making out a human shape at a few yards.

After the business of feeding the owls was over we went into the house. There were hens all over the floor and a woman covered like an Arab in black from head to foot was washing out a tub of what I took to be cow's intestines. We sat – uncomfortably so far as I was concerned – on low stools at a table a foot high, and presently the woman left her tripes and brought a tray with some eight or ten tiny glasses of red wine on it. This was the local system; one offered and accepted hospitality by downing a number of glasses of red wine, so, reasonably enough, the glasses had to be small. We sat under a popular wartime picture of a flying monk winging down to earth with an Italian airforce pilot just rescued from a burning plane in his arms. Minasola used a large red handkerchief to wipe the rheum from his eyelids. He seemed much aged since our last meeting, and between sentences his mouth drooped to display his tongue.

I told him about my journalistic friends, and he thought it only natural that being in Sicily they should want to see Giuliano. What paper did they work for? he asked, and I told him the *Tribune*, and that Nancy took pictures for *Life*. This piece of news filled him with excitement. *Life* was his favourite magazine, he said. 'If your friend has any copies she can spare I would be pleased to have them,' he said. 'I like to cut the pictures out.'

'When your friends go to Montelepre,' he said, 'they must ask for the Cavaliere Santo Fiore.' He managed a weak smile. I knew this already. This was the Sicilian equivalent of the army chain of command, and I knew that the Cavaliere was the Montelepre man of respect and it would be the accepted practice for all contacts with the bandit to be made through him. An exchange of small presents – the equivalent of the African 'dash' – was a matter of protocol on an occasion such as this. Although he almost certainly could not sign his name, I gave Minasola a fountain pen, with which he seemed happy, and he presented me with a large goat's cheese in return.

5

THIS WAS A TUESDAY and as it occurred to me that the journey to Montelepre might upset my arrangements with the Marchesina for the Thursday, I sent a local boy round to the palace with a message explaining that I might be held up, and received the astringent reply. 'Play it your way. *Cui di spiranza campa, disparatu mori.*' (He who lives in hope, dies in despair.)

We set off next morning at six. Rod's final plan was that if things went well in Montelepre he and Nancy would stay up there for several days. I did not wish to be away more than two days from Palma di Cava, so it was decided to take the two cars, and having helped them in whatever way I could it was agreed that I should leave them and drive back in my old Bianchi.

The road to Montelepre crossed the wildest and least known part of the island. This was the first week in May and down on the coast summer had turned on its full blast, but the interior could have been the highlands of Scotland, an emerald landscape of rolling mountains and glens, and there were foxes bobbing up their heads in the heather and eagles spiralling in the sky. Rod held us up to rush off into a cave and measure the depth of midden accumulation, claiming in a matter of ten minutes to have discovered evidence of neolithic occupation. Apart from such occasional delays chargeable to scientific curiosity, the pace was slow. Rod's problem was to skirt the innumerable pot-holes and avoid damage to his springs. He was weighted down, he mentioned, not only with souvenirs and a month's supply of Spam, but almost enough spares to rebuild the car.

We stopped at four villages on the way where Nancy fed the cats. (The people in these mountain villages were not so hungry as those of the towns, so there were a few about.) This was something she always came prepared to do, she said, when they travelled in under-developed countries. As soon as we stopped in the little square of the first village a number of emaciated cats gathered as if in response to some instinct around the Dodge, and Nancy opened a large can of cat food and began to feed them.

'They're really beautiful,' she said. 'Did you ever see a cat with eyes like these before? Don't you get a wham out of the kind of delicate way they take their food?'

Such was their enthusiasm for Sicily that not even a Sicilian cat could set a foot wrong. She had ready a dozen or so blue plastic saucers and the food was spooned into these, and they were set out around the car. Despite the general theory that animals were colour-blind, Nancy had proved by experiment that they approached the food more eagerly when it was offered in a receptacle of this colour. After she fed them the cats began to dash about in all directions, startlingly invigorated by whatever the food had been. Either she or Rod mentioned at this point that they had become attracted to an oriental religion known as El Bab (the gateway) which enjoined compassion for all forms of life. 'We must share our bounty with the animals,' Nancy said, and I liked her and Rod too much to raise the question of lack of compassion shown to the animals in the can.

When she had finished feeding the cats, Nancy went round making friends with the old people sitting in their doorways, snapping them with her Rolleiflex and trying to make conversation in phrase-book Italian which they pretended most convincingly to understand. About one in ten of them had never left their village. It was doubtful if any had ever seen a woman in slacks before; certainly they had never been approached by one wanting to photograph them. They accepted these experiences with a cultivated indifference. I suspected that had I levelled a camera at them they might have excused themselves softly and gone indoors, but when Nancy turned on her charm and her smile, they were overwhelmed.

This pleasant pattern of activity with the snapshotting and the cats was reproduced in each of the small villages, and again when we reached Montelepre.

We parked the two cars in the small space cleared by earthquakes confidently known as the Piazza and went in search of the Cavaliere. He was already known to me by reputation as the man who, at the time of the Abyssinian war, had opened a canning factory at Mogadishu to process the flesh of abandoned camels, subsequently marketed at great profit under the label 'Sahara Cow'. His main claim to fame was based upon the way he had duped Vittorio Emmanuele into accepting an ugly and spurious cross he asserted once hung on the bosom of the emperor Haile Selassie, and the King had been unable to get out of conferring a knighthood of the Crown of Italy on him in return. Exaggerated rumours flew about concerning the Cavaliere's crimes, committed in early life at a time when, as the local expression went, 'he was making his bones'. Nowadays he lived comfortably off the fear he was said once to have inspired.

'He may come as a surprise,' I told my American friends. We had been talking about men of respect. 'This is a local phenomenon which I can't explain and I don't know anyone who can. When the King visited Sicily Santo Fiore patted him on the back and told him he might as well have left his police behind because he, Santo Fiore, would see to it that he came to no harm.'

'But is this man like one of our gangsters back home?' Nancy asked.

'Not from what I've heard. We'll probably find that he's exceedingly pleasant and polite. He's an old man, an asthmatic and he has difficulty in walking, but make no mistake he rules in Montelepre.'

'How about Giuliano? How does he come into this?'

'It's hard to say. Giuliano may be something quite new. Traditionally men of respect use bandits to maintain their power, and then get rid of them when they see them as no longer being of any use. Time will tell.'

The first person we asked for the Cavaliere took us to his house, built in the style of an Alpine chalet in a large, overgrown garden. The rooms, this man told us, were in such a mess due to the notorious idleness of his staff, that he would almost certainly decide to receive us in the garden, and this proved to be the case. Two servants brought him out, one supporting him under each arm. The Cavaliere seemed to have dressed himself hurriedly for the occasion, with the star and sash of his order over a crumpled jacket, worn with baggy trousers gaping at the waist, and carpet slippers – one cut away to relieve the pressure on a gouty toe. A white goatee straggled from the Cavaliere's chin, and his expression was indulgent and benign. A third servant followed carrying an armchair into which he was slowly lowered when he tottered into our presence. His efforts had turned him puce in the face, and he struggled for a while to get breath while one of his men tried to fan air into his mouth. As soon as he had recovered he was affability itself, signalling to be tugged into an upright position in order to be able to bend over and kiss Nancy's hand. There were ritual gifts to be exchanged. I gave the Cavaliere a half pound of bacon, and Rod brought along a selection of breakfast cereals which delighted him. Rod and I received illuminated parchments with the Cavaliere's biographical details and Nancy a mounted Abyssinian scarab of fearsome appearance.

One had to be absolutely frank with men like the Cavaliere who had an intuitive understanding of human motives. I explained the facts exactly as they were – that my two American friends were journalists and that Minasola had sent us in the hope that he might agree to fixing an interview with Giuliano. I used the bait of *Life* magazine once again, and it turned out that, like Minasola, the Cavaliere was much impressed by this publication. 'Sure, yes, OK, you can see him,' he said. He had picked up his English by association with the troops, threw an OK into every sentence, and was often difficult to understand.

A discussion followed in which we were sometimes at cross-purposes through the Cavaliere's habit of confusing words of opposite meanings, such as good with bad. When he said, 'the bandits gave us a good time, OK?' he meant that they had made life difficult. Giuliano had taken off the pressure, although in so far as it was possible to follow the Cavaliere's argument he had now adopted an inadmissible reformism. 'This guy says quit rustling cattle or I'm going to blow your heads off. So they stop rustling, OK. Now he says give your dough to the poor. Who for fuck he is? We got five hundred priests here making us pray and go to church. We don't need him to break our balls for Chrissake.'

Watching from his web in the depths of his untidy house the Cavaliere probably knew all of Giuliano's movements and most of his intentions. It was to be gathered from his account – even if not expressed in so many words – that Giuliano's sudden conversion to good works, while popular with the depressed five-sixths of the population of Montelepre and in the surrounding area half-seriously referred to as his kingdom, had alarmed the rich, including many of his separatist backers.

At that moment Giuliano was away with his band levelling incomes and dealing out instant justice in the few square miles under his control. The Cavaliere said that he was not expected back until the next morning, and pressed us while awaiting his return to stay in his house. A problem arose. He had the reputation of a man never able to throw anything away, and he admitted – as confirmed later by Rod and Nancy's description – that every room was piled high with the potentially useful litter of years, from hundreds of empty boxes to innumerable cooking pots with small holes in their bottoms, and defective clocks. Apart from the room in which he himself slept there was only one other, with narrow lanes through the accumulation of surplus articles leading eventually to a bed. The experience was one that Rod and Nancy were happy to accept. There were the germs of possibility here for a piece for one or other of the magazines. Nancy got out her Rolleiflex there and then and took several shots of the Cavaliere, indulgent and beatific against the background of datura blooms and piled-up cardboard boxes in the garden. This gave me an easy way of escape, and shortly afterwards, having fixed a time for a meeting next morning, I excused myself and found a room for the night over a local bar.

This trip had offered the opportunity to contact an old friend, Placido.

'Back again, I can't believe my eyes,' he said. 'What brought you here of all places?'

'A couple of Americans wanted to see Giuliano.'

A slight movement of the eyebrows and a shrug suggested the question, why?

'Who's looking after them?' he wanted to know.

'Fiore.'

'That should be an experience.'

Placido Calandra, a devotee of astronomy, had taken his telescope, left Palma and moved up here to the mountains where the air was exceptionally dry and clear. He saw in the contemplation of the stars a swing of the pendulum after two wartime years as an interpreter spent in the pursuit of female officers of the Allied armed forces, out of infatuation with their uniforms rather than their feminine charms. There had been so many of them that he admitted later with regret that, rather than of faces and bodies, his memory in those days of dearth was of tunics and skirts of various styles, cut and colour, and their austere but appetizing adjuncts by way of service-issue undergarments.

We dined on beans in the spartan surroundings I had come to expect in the house of a Sicilian intellectual.

'Quiet up here after Palma,' I said.

'And rudimentary,' he said. He nodded in the direction of the furniture put together by some local carpenter with the bright screw heads gleaming in the freshly planed wood. A tap in the corner dripped on unwashed plates in a shallow porcelain sink let into the floor for the purpose of washing the feet.

'Remember the old days in the field hospital at Gela?' he asked. 'What were you in for?'

'Malaria.'

'Malaria. That's it. It wipes out your blood corpuscles,' he said. 'You'd have missed half the fun. The American nurses in the casualty wards were terrific. One theory was they were excited by the smell of blood. There was one called Veronica, maybe it was Virginia. Something beginning with a V. Heavy drinker like the rest of them. "Kiss me here," she said, and there was a distinct taste of gin. Hard to believe it ever happened. I've practically retired from the world up here. Perhaps I wore myself out.'

'You've probably matured.'

'Which is another way of saying the same thing. The outlook on life in this place is very restricted,' he said. 'An Englishwoman comes up from Gela once a month and takes on all-comers at the back of the pub where you're staying. She's quite expensive; not too beautiful either, but strong. I save up and have myself thrashed once in a while. My bones practically come through the skin.' He smiled apologetically with a display of teeth coloured by malnutrition like a matured meerschaum pipe. 'If only there'd been some way of holding something in reserve from the old days,' he said. 'The stars are my consolation, and I seem to have moved closer to them since I've been here, and of course they've kept me alive.'

'You can actually make a living out of astronomy?'

'Astrology. You've probably heard the Sicilians don't understand hope, and it struck me that if only I could promote it there must be a market for it. They've always gone in for horoscopes but in a negative sort of way, by which I mean that if the indications were bad on a particular day they kept their heads down or went to bed. I set out to sell them hope and at the moment I'm doing syndicated hopeful horoscopes for twenty-two newspapers. The thing's taken off.'

'Is it all bogus?'

'Not entirely, although I started off on the assumption that it was. Scientifically my charts are as accurate as I can make them. I've often been taken by surprise to see how my predictions work out. There must be something in it.'

We moved to the window where his telescope mounted on a tripod pointed through the window towards the sky over Montelepre, an ugly township so refined and dignified by distance that it might have been the meticulous background to a cinquecento painting of some biblical scene of revelation and grace.

'The more I study the stars,' Placido said, 'the greater the fascination they hold over me. I've calculated there are fourteen thousand within range of the telescope from where we stand. In Montelepre, people don't see them, they only barely realize they're there. Everything is settled in advance. I stop a man in the street and put in a little propaganda. "Do you understand that the stars have an influence on your life?" I say to him. "Well, I imagine there's nothing I can do about it," he usually says. And then I explain to him that he can and give him a free introductory horoscope. "Study this," I say, "and it will turn you into a happier man." I see it as a sort of crusade.'

I decided on a night cap at the bar where I was staying, and learned in the course of conversation with the owner a piece of news that Placido would be sorry to hear.

'We're the victims of interference,' the man said. 'This place has nothing to offer anyone in the way of entertainment but what I've been able to provide until now.'

He took me behind the bar into the comfortably furnished back room where Placido had gone to have the Englishwoman beat the living daylights out of him once a month. 'You could come here for a quiet drink, sit and hold hands with a girl, look at a French movie. Anybody would think it was a whorehouse.' He was complaining of the action of Giuliano's newly formed 'moral attitude' squad, who had closed it down on the previous day, at the same time confiscating for destruction calendars put out by cigarette manufacturers, featuring girls in the standard provocative poses which were the only form of art accessible to the people of Montelepre.

He had started as a supporter of Giuliano's. The bandit had made a start with his good works by issuing an order that no child should appear barefoot on the streets, and had distributed several hundred pairs of boots to see to it that this did not happen. Next he had got himself into the newspapers by providing dowries for girls of poor families. 'All well and good,' the man said.

While we were talking, two young men came in and the owner went back to polishing his counter. The newcomers wore the ordinary cheap, badly made shirt and trousers that were all a peasant could afford, along with boots of exceptional quality, with attached gaiters buttoning half way up to the knee, of the type issued to the US infantry. They both had a well-scrubbed and shaved appearance, cheerful expressions. They shook hands with the owner and then with me, and ordered soft drinks of a kind made from herbs and mountain berries, which left, as I had discovered, an after-taste of chewed pencils. When they had drunk up they shook hands with us again, wished us good evening, and went off. These were the two men, the owner told me, who had visited him on the previous day, who had returned, he supposed, to make sure that he was not backsliding.

Their visit seemed to inflame the owner, who wanted to know where this kind of thing was going to stop. Giuliano had cleaned the place up, ordering the mountains of rubbish lying in the streets, upon which citizens actually grew vegetables, to be carted away. He could see no reason, he said, in such an action. From this Giuliano had gone on to impose fines for the common practice of defecating in the roadway. 'There's nowhere to go in this town to have a shit these days,' he said. 'They're taking our freedom away.'

6

I WENT TO BED in the cubicle over the bar, anaesthetized and plunged instantly into deep slumber by the thin mountain air. In these small towns silence descends with the backdrop of night, and dawn awakes the instant clamour of the day. It was hardly five when I pushed open the window, and looked down on a streaming of men on mules or in carts on their way to the mountain terraces and the fields. A sight that astonished me was the spectacle of a gang of men whose urban style of clothing showed them not to be peasants, at work shovelling up a large mound of ancient manure before loading it onto handcarts to be carried away. This, rather than unusual, was revolutionary – the theory being that dung was allowed to accumulate in the streets to deaden the rattle of passing carts, and where there were sizeable drifts of it in out-of-the-way corners it was frequently used to grow vegetables of exceptional quality.

I was speculating on the reason for this operation when Rod and Nancy cantered into sight, disbursing so much evident energy in these surroundings where it was normal for it to be carefully conserved. I shouted and waved to them and then went down to let them in. They were bursting – almost incoherent – with the night's news. 'Listen,' Rod said. 'Can you imagine the situation where one man can take over the water supply of a town this size? Well, he certainly can here. Every drop of water consumed here had to be bought from Fiore. That was until Giuliano took over.'

'Personally I don't find that any stranger than a man owning all the land around a town,' Nancy said.

'Land's a nice thing to own,' Rod said. 'Water's essential. This town gets its drinking water from a single spring, and now Giuliano's given it back to the people it belongs to.'

'Which is unlikely to have increased his popularity with Fiore,' I said.

'I would agree with you there, but it was something had to be done. Now people can drink all they want, and even hose down the streets once in a while. Giuliano is out to clean this town up, and I mean literally. Nancy and I ran into a guy organizing volunteers on our way down. We told him we'd regard it as a privilege to contribute a little of our time and labour, but he didn't appear to take us seriously.'

The owner of the bar dragged himself yawning and rubbing his eyes out of the room where Placido had been accustomed to have himself flogged, and Rod pounced on him, thrust a packet of decaffeinated coffee into his hands and gestured in the direction of his espresso machine.

'So how was it at Fiore's place?' I asked.

59

'It was the raw material of experience. I have to get to a phone to talk to *Esquire* about this. This man is so fat he can't lie down to sleep. He sleeps strapped into a chair tilted back maybe at an angle of forty-five degrees. You're not going to believe this, but he has a perpetual motion thing worked out with white rats and wheels. This is a room you could play soft-ball in, with hundreds of white rats running about in cages all round the walls. They've learned to do without sleep and he has a system for feeding them on the run. He spends his life watching them. He says it gives him a sensation of ultimate power. Listen, to go to the toilet, you sit in a kind of curtained armchair and it swings you over a stream. Fifty yards further down you see the women washing their clothes in it.'

'Mr Fiore is treated very badly by his servants,' Nancy said. 'He doesn't seem to have any control over them.'

'They rob him blind,' Rod said. 'And they tell you this guy is the biggest noise in this part of Sicily. I have to write up my notes before I forget any of this.'

The owner came with the coffee. Nancy fumbled in a bag and lined up several packets of breakfast cereals. Next came an episode of the kind that continually rekindled my admiration for these Americans. There was no milk but at that moment a flock of goats was being driven past. Nancy ran out and immediately borrowed one of these from its owner, milked it on the spot, and was back within five minutes. I was overwhelmed by her enterprise. What spirit. What effrontery. What charm.

'The man actually called his goat over by name,' Nancy said. 'Claudia.' She couldn't get over it.

'They're rather closer to animals than we are,' I said. This opinion seemed to surprise them both, and Nancy probably felt it unreasonable that people who never in any circum-

60

stances fed cats should be seen as having a closer relationship with them than those who did.

'The man of respect who fixed up this trip is crazy about goats,' I said. 'He's said to sit and watch them for hours.'

'Does he kill and eat them?' Rod asked.

'I'm sure he does.'

Rod shook his head.

'They have an annual tunny fishing near Palma di Cava. The fishermen take barrel organs in the boats and play to the fish to calm their nerves, then they stab them to death. You could practically swim in the blood. The fish are supposed to prefer Verdi.'

'Fascinating country,' Rod said. 'I mean does it still come strange to you?'

'In a way,' I said. 'They can still take me by surprise. But that's the beauty of it, and thinking about it I suspect that's one of the reasons I'm here.'

It had been left with Fiore that Rod and Nancy would present themselves at his house at about midday to be ceremonially conducted into Giuliano's presence as soon as he returned to Montelepre. My friends were determined to learn all that was to be known about the life of the town, and I was pressed into accompanying them on a fact-finding tour. While Nancy, virtually squelching charm, flattered and cajoled the old, shoved chewing gum into children's mouths, exposed a half dozen rolls of film and kept an eye open for appealing cats, Rod, notebook in hand and brow furrowed with intellectual curiosity, began his investigation. This involved me in an interpretative role I found embarrassing because Rod kept up a quick fire of questions most of which seemed to be profoundly unimportant and irrelevant. Nevertheless it had to be admitted that the locals

– avid probably for a moment's distraction from the boredom of small-town life – were delighted to co-operate.

'John, do me a favour. Ask this guy if his mother or any of
his family has goitre. Maybe he can say what the percentage
of sufferers from goitre is in this town.'

'I don't know the word for goitre.'

'Pity. Well, no sweat. This lady here looks kind of easy to
talk to. Would you tell her we'd be very glad to know from
her the weights of her children at birth.'

'Rod,' I said, 'I don't want to do this. Besides difficulty
with the vocabulary, I'm bored.'

Happily it is impossible to spend more than a few minutes
in such a place as Montelepre without running into a native
returned from some years of exile in the States who has con-
tracted a reverence for miscellaneous information, and
within a short time, and to my relief, such a man picked up
our scent and came homing in. Rod's only problem here, I
could see, would be to get in a question edgeways. However,
it gave me an excuse to detach myself. We made a rough
arrangement to meet back in the square between two and
three after the hoped-for interview. I left Nancy breaking
down the resistance to photography of an old man with a
hare lip, and Rod and our new friend discussing the straw
content in local bricks, and went back to the square with the
intention of picking up the car and driving into the surrounding mountain villages in search of any of the old music
I might be able to record.

We had left the cars parked side by side and Rod seemed
to have got over his fear of leaving the Dodge unattended as
there had been no suggestion that someone should be found,
as in Palma, to sleep in the cabin. Somewhat to my surprise
I noticed by the tyre marks in the skin of rubbish awaiting
removal in this part of the square, that the car had been

backed out from its original position, driven off and then returned. It was only to be supposed that the Americans had gone off on a sight-seeing trip before settling down for the night in Fiore's house.

I set out for Sagana, a few miles away, where Placido had told me that the old music was most likely to have survived, but was hardly out of Montelepre when I was forced to pull into the side to make way for an extraordinary collection of men streaming up towards the town. In these days there were strolling players to be seen on the roads of Italy and Sicily and they were distinguished by their strange and even grotesque appearance; men who were excessively tall and thin, others so small as to be almost dwarfs. Any physical deformity in the way of big heads and lantern jaws seemed to be favoured among these groups, and they often dressed themselves in odd garments forming part of military uniforms of any of the armies that had campaigned in Italy. These men were just such a collection, differing only in their appearance from the players in their, if possible, more unkempt appearance and in the miscellany of firearms they carried at the trail, over their shoulders, or underarm in hunter style. They scuttled past in an uproar of laughter and horseplay, the small men almost running to keep up with the tall ones. There could have been a hundred of them and it was not until half of them had passed that I realized that this tatterdemalion collection of jugglers and clowns were the Giuliano band – most famous outlaws of the century – and that the man I had glimpsed briefly at their head was the bandit himself. I cast my mind back to the picture taken by the photographer from Palma who had perhaps been more skilful than I had supposed. Giuliano's brother Vincenzo who worked at a filling station in Palermo had once been pointed out to me and as far as I had had time to record the appearance of the man at the head of the band the similarity between the brothers was exceptional. Both Vincenzo and Giuliano had the faces of men fated to spend their days filling tanks and polishing windscreens. In Giuliano's case, almost fated, for he had killed a policeman trying to arrest him for some trivial offence, and greatness of a kind had been thrust upon him.

I waited until the last straggler went by and the outcry, the whistles and the catcalls fell away to silence, then started off again, and half an hour later I was in Sagana, where until recently the speciality had been male singers with voices like women who bandaged their throats over the vocal cords to produce a strange warbling delivery, described by the chairman of the commune as 'very unmelodious, and no longer in demand'. The chairman said, 'You see what finished us off was the American base just up the road. They gave us everything we asked for, so why bother to sing? We have a proverb which says, "He who sings frightens away his fear." With our kind American friends looking after us we had nothing to be afraid of any more. There was a group of men who blew rams' horns and banged a drum, but they've given up too. The Americans presented us with a radio when they left, and who's going to blow on rams' horns or play the fiddle when they can switch on the radio? You might say they killed us with kindness. It's something we've never recovered from.'

I got back to Montelepre in good time and found Rod and Nancy waiting in the bar. Rod was twitching and blinking with excitement, and his hands, completely out of control, groped constantly after small objects on the table such as coffee cups and an ashtray, in an effort to use up a particle of energy.

'So you saw the great man?'

'We certainly did,' Rod said, 'and let me say he's great by any standard. Much much bigger than expected. A reformer.'

'Does giving away dowries come under the heading of reforms?'

'He gives away dowries, yes, and that's good propaganda. What he's really out to do is break the hold of the banks. Let's just suppose you need a loan for any purpose in one of these villages. What are they going to charge in the way of interest? Fifty-five percent, maybe more. Does that strike you as iniquitous, John? It does me.'

'All the same I'd go careful about taking on the banks if I were him.'

'He can do it,' Nancy said. 'Because this is a guy who can do anything he wants. You can't have any conception of how big this man is until you've seen him and talked with him. I know you're going to tell me he has no education. It's something he's been able to by-pass. He's instinctive. He's been granted the gift of perception, and that's what counts. If anyone can emerge victorious in the struggle against Mammon, this is the man.'

'I wish him well,' I said. 'It's time someone took the banks on.'

'Let me tell you about the way he lives,' Nancy said. 'He's chosen the simplest possible way of life. He goes around in a cheap shirt and pants and sleeps on the floor. The food people like us consume in one day would last him a week. In winter he goes up to the mountain peaks and cleanses himself in the snow. For me that's a religious attitude. That's something like communing with God. He said he avoids the distraction of material possessions. In other words he lives like he's poor.'

'The fact he's made the headlines has had no effect on

him,' Rod said. 'You go to see him and he could be anybody. "Come right in," he says. He grabs you by the hand and gives you a big smile. "You want to ask me anything," he says, "go right ahead. My time's at your disposal," or words to that effect. His English is not too great but somehow he gets his meaning across. You follow what he's saying about his plans for the future of Sicily. You could say in a way it's like listening to a child. I mean he has a restricted knowledge of the language, and yet it all comes over.'

'My impression is his mother has played a large part in the formation of his ideas,' Nancy said. 'It was our privilege to be allowed to meet her today, a middle-aged peasant lady of great warmth and charm. I was permitted to take a number of photographs of mother and son, both separately and together. Giuliano told us that even when he had been forced to take to the mountains his mother had always found some way of following him, so that they were rarely separated. The local people tell you she had a vision when she was a young girl – the Madonna, I guess – who told her that the son she would give birth to would cast down the devil from the mountain tops. This is something he doesn't want to talk about. "The devil is not up there on the mountains," he says. "He's right here in this town."'

'This man's problem is how to deal with the goddam mess he's inherited,' Rod said. 'You can't build up without pulling down first. What's been done about all the fat cats left over from Fascism? What's been done about all these millions of dollars made on the black market? The answer is nothing. This is a corrupt country and only somebody like Giuliano can take on that corruption. You've probably heard of the way he deals with enemies of society he considers beyond redemption.'

'Yes, he shoots them.'

'This was one of the problems he discussed with us. Out here it takes two years to bring a case to trial. You can bribe the prosecuting attorney and bribe the police. If a guy has given evidence he always retracts it and the case is dismissed. Democratic justice as you or I understand it doesn't exist.'

'He told us that his decision to impose the death penalty was the hardest he had ever made,' Nancy said. 'There's going to be a public demonstration of the people's justice this afternoon.'

'That will be the fourth or fifth,' I said. 'Who is it to be this time?'

'A big food speculator,' Rod said. 'You can say I'm opposed to the death penalty as a matter of principle, but when people are still literally starving by the thousand this is a case when I'm inclined to make an exception. Giuliano has offered Nancy facilities to take photographs.'

'Did you take him up?' I asked her.

'Why certainly,' Nancy said. 'Of course.'

'It could be a gruesome experience,' I said.

The remark seemed to surprise her. She shook her head. 'It wouldn't be,' she said. 'The only problem might arise from coping with a new set of technical problems. When you're involved in a demanding job you put everything out of your mind but the technicalities involved. Things like composition, shutter speeds and using the right lens.' I noticed suddenly that the soft, rich voice had taken on an edge of crispness and that Nancy's face had changed. Suddenly she had slipped into a brisk new role. Professionalism had entered her like an invading spirit. The moment recalled snippets of breakfast talk, when she had spoken of her remote background. The camp at Moctezuma was full of Indians with nothing to do but scrounge. 'The pastor used to hand out plates of rice and say, "When you eat this remember God wants us to work. He wants us to give of our best. Remember he blesses our labours." I guess that sank in.' The pastor had made another convert, the altars of Huit-zilpochtli and the gods of corn and rain had been cast down to be replaced by that of the deity of motivation and endeavour. She seemed to race after my thought. 'Work is a kind of religion with me,' Nancy said. 'I'm only happy when I'm giving all I've got to my job.' With exhortation and rice had the pastor conquered. In Nancy nothing but a husk of the grand fecklessness of the Indian people remained.

Rod's response to the uplift of work was predictably the same. 'As a writer you have to take the same point of view. You set your sights on professional detachment. At first you will yourself not to feel, then it comes naturally. You're writing for an anonymous face who wants to know what happened, and after that nothing. The great American public is about as liberal-minded as a dinosaur and anything that offends the reader is going to make him reach for the telephone and cancel his subscription. The only thing he can't hit you with are the facts, and that's what you give him. Facts on the rocks. He has to feel he was there himself with nothing on his mind but the football score and his next lay. If he does that you're the kind of journalist I aspire to be, and if not you should be selling insurance.'

The execution had been set for four in the afternoon, but was subject to all the hitches and delays to be expected on such occasions. We found ourselves on waste ground outside the village where the peasants had butchered some tyrannical officials at the time of Garibaldi's takeover, and had themselves been massacred by troops. A low wall protruded from the weeds, and a solemn inscription testified to the tragedy of those who had lined up before it to face the guns. It had been a cenotaph, and now once again it was to be returned to its original use, and I found it sad and also macabre that it should have been decided to protect this wall with its inscription in such a conscientious fashion with the sandbags it must have been difficult to procure.

It was at this point that I experienced once again a feeling I had noticed when confronted with certain dramatic experiences in the past, that what was happening was a little unreal. There was an unhurried matter-of-factness about the scene, unsuited to a solemn occasion, and little evidence of organization or purpose. What should have been in its way an enormity, was nothing. Perhaps this was a self-protective trick I had developed to deal with such situations. Rod and Nancy had gone off armoured in their professionalism, and I placed myself defensively at the back of a group of countrymen, in their black, wedding-funeral suits and sparkling shoes, who by their relaxed and indifferent postures gave the impression that they had just happened to be there. They chatted comfortably, sharing a loaf of bread, and somewhere just out of sight a barrel organ rattled its background of shallow music for this informal encounter with death. Rod had agreed to occupy the waiting chair placed before the wall for a moment, so that Nancy could focus up and choose the appropriate lens. Behind the wall grew enormously tall weeds with birds fluttering in their seed heads, and several of the grotesquely uniformed men I had met on the road to Sagana that morning had wandered away to urinate among them. There was no urgency, no hushed voices, no strung-up nerves. No one had been drawn to this place by morbid impulse. The townspeople around me chewed on their breadcrusts, picked their teeth, yawned and asked each other the time.

A black car ornamented with carved wooden flowers came bumping up, stopped, and three men and a young priest got out. Since two men were wearing nondescript uniforms, and the third was not, it was clear that he was the prisoner. Otherwise all three looked remarkably alike, and appeared equally unexcited. Prisoners in Italy are normally transported from place to place with a great display of chains, but here there were none. The condemned man, his captors and the priest formed a little discussion group. Certain matters were being explained to the man I took to be the prisoner, as to an initiate in any ceremony, and he seemed to express his understanding and compliance with fluid hand-gestures and a shrug of the shoulders. The four then walked briskly towards the awaiting chair, and the prisoner took his seat, readjusted the angle of his hat, folded his arms and waited. Up in front the three bandits had sauntered into position and were tinkering with their guns. I recognized one of them as a man I had seen on the Sagana road that morning, but noted that all three were now armed with the latest American light carbines. To the right of the man in the chair Nancy peered into the focusing screen of her Rolleiflex. The barrel organ had gone silent, a hundred birds twittered as they stripped away at the seedheads, a dog barked. I went back to the Bianchi, got in, and drove off.

I made brief reference to this episode in my second situation report, accompanying the bare bones of fact with an informal letter to the Colonel.

It turned out that there was no problem about making the trip to Giuliano's kingdom at Montelepre. The Steins were granted their interview, both of them succumbing instantly to the well-known charm. I find it quite mysterious that this basically ignorant man could have captured and enslaved the popular imagination. He is widely credited with the gifts of perfume and bilocation – technicalities employed in local hagiology – meaning that their possessor smells of roses and can be in two places at once. They sell pictures in Montelepre showing him in the vestments of a Byzantine saint, sometimes with his swarthy forty-five-year-old mother appearing in the background as a simpering girl of seventeen, usually with blue eyes and fair hair. According to the ballad singers he has become the lover of the Duchess of Pratamena, but this is repudiated by most of his followers who claim that he is free from carnal desire, although able to put a woman in the family way without actual contact. Another five years, and they'll be having him fly through the air like a bird. (If he lasts five years, I thought, but best not discourage the Colonel by suggesting that's highly unlikely.)

Peasants are always on the lookout for new gods and this is just an up-to-date, black-market version of one. I suspect the moneyed classes are not quite so happy with him as they were. This was to be their champion against the Reds and now they see him giving dowries away, stuffing banknotes into destitute widows' hands and letting people off their rents, which smells a bit too much like socialism. Imagine how the Sicilian banks feel about him. They backed him and a separate Sicily because they thought that would be the best way to get rid of their Roman competitors, and now he tells them he expects them to cut their lending rates from thirty to five percent.

The military situation is no longer any secret. Giuliano has been named Colonel-in-Chief of the separatist forces (largely bandits) in the west of the island, and Concetto Gallo of those in the east and not far from this town.

Many of these too are reported to be fugitives from justice. The weakness of the movement lies in the wide geographical separation of the two fronts, added to the conflicting personalities of the two commanders who are said to view each other with suspicion probably mingled with contempt. Giuliano would like to put an end to feudalism. Gallo sees it as not going half far enough in its management of the destinies of the poor and proposes to restore their innate nobility of soul by the abolition of all methods of tilling the soil except the archaic nail-plough, by a low diet of maize gruel, early rising, early marriage and prayer. This is clearly not what Giuliano has in mind. The question is whether these two men, one a guerrilla fighter who claims never to have slept a single night in a city, the other a capricious and eccentric millionaire who believes that all military activity should be modelled on Caesar's campaigns, can ever successfully link up.

On rereading what I had written it seemed to me that the Colonel – clearly drawn to the cause of Sicilian separatism – might find it depressing. I was about to throw in a piece of waiter's gossip. It was hardly more than a whisper behind raised hands, with not even the strength in it to be classified as a rumour. *The miners look like caving in*, somebody had said. No more than that. Certainly nothing for the official report; nothing to influence in any way the Churchill–Truman policy. From the Colonel's point of view it would sound like bad news, and I decided to spare him unnecessary alarm.

7

THE ARRANGEMENT WAS that I should pick up the Marchesina round the corner from the palace, out of sight of her neighbours who spent much of their time at their windows, starved in the austere landscape of their inner lives of a happening of any kind upon which to build a shred of fantasy.

She was an hour late, and to my consternation the Seaweed Eater was with her, wrapped up despite the heat in moth-eaten furs, her head trussed under a winged hat in the style of early motoring in readiness for a journey.

'What's she doing here?' I asked.

'She's coming with us.'

'There's no furniture to be shifted.'

'She wants to come and I can't afford to offend her.'

The conversation was in English, which the Marchesina preferred to speak at any time, but the Seaweed Eater must have guessed what was going on, and she glowered suspicion.

'Is there no way of bribing her?'

'No, and please don't try it. I don't want her to walk out on me.'

I gave in, pulled open the dicky seat and agile as ever the Seaweed Eater hoisted herself in, settled with a shifting of her hips like a hen on her eggs, and adjusted her amazing hat. There was triumph in her smile. I tried to kiss the Marchesina but she backed away smiling. 'Not while she's got her eye on us,' she said. 'We have all the time.' She was radiant as ever, costumed for the *Medea*, shod in golden sandals and wearing earrings stolen from an Etruscan tomb, a strikingly unsuitable ensemble for a hard ride in a small car over roads coated with a half inch of laterite dust. We started off but I stopped after a few miles to see what had happened to the Seaweed Eater. 'Are you all right?' I called to her and her eyes opened cautiously, the taut maquillage of ochrous powder cracked, starting tiny landslides on her cheeks. She croaked what might have been a protest.

'When do we get her off our hands?' I asked the Marchesina.

'Tonight if we're lucky,' she said. 'She refuses to be left alone.'

We pushed on towards Marinella, a small manic seaside town of a kind only to be found in Sicily with a wild mixture of crenellations, Moorish arches, stained glass, crazy pavement, and broken statuary. People went there to fornicate surreptitiously in the vicinity of a ruined temple of Venus, to gape at an angel's footprint in the rock, to cuddle the polished shaft of a prehistoric phallus and sometimes to commit suicide by sliding down an increasingly steep grassy slope which finally precipitated them into a deep sea saturated with the benign magic of coral.

Marinella was also famous for its small black crabs.

'It's crabs for dinner,' the Marchesina said.

'How do they serve them?'

'Alive,' she said.

'I'll leave them to you and the Seaweed Eater,' I told her.

The reason the Marchesina had chosen Marinella for our excursion was her determination that we should occupy the largest bed in the land, once the property of a Bourbon king, and said to be able easily to accommodate ten persons. The manager of the hotel in which this was housed seemed aloof until he had studied the Marchesina's entry (read upside down) occupying one and a half lines listing titles long divested of anything but a whispered echo of past glory. After this he became cowed and ingratiating, addressed the Marchesina as Signora Marchesa instead of *voi* and immediately agreed to show us the bed.

In a country where real power had always been advertised by the size of the bed a man slept in, this piece of furniture was astonishing, and it was quite certain that however fitful their slumber might have been ten persons could have slept in it. It was clear too, since this was claimed to have been a royal bed, that the royalty of the eighteenth century could not bear to be wholly separated even at night from the serious and stimulating preoccupations of the hunt, because the side and back curtains were richly embroidered with scenes of huntsmen at their sport and monstrous dogs tearing at the flanks and throats of deer.

'Who did you say the king was?' the Marchesina asked.

'His Majesty Ferdinand IV, King of Naples and Sicily.'

I made a note to tell her the story of his courtiers licking his forearm.

'How did they get the bed into the room?'

'They removed the window and much of the wall. Lord Nelson asked for a copy to be made for his palace at Brontë, but none of the rooms was large enough to accommodate it.'

'There is a fusty smell in here. Please open the windows.' The Marchesina's manner had become peremptory. I had noticed before that as soon as she was removed from Palma and its warning reminders of aristocratic decline, she became imperious and even difficult. We stood close to a gilt mirror carved with glum-looking cupids. She ran the tip of a finger up the curve of a snub nose, and inspected it severely. 'I shall take the room,' she said. 'Be so good as to have it dusted.'

The room was clearly a show-piece, not intended for occupation. The man spread his hands in supplication, embarrassment, then defeat, and finally went off to find a maid.

The Seaweed Eater had been briefly got rid of first to clean herself up after the journey, and then – with no evidence of reluctance on her part – to scour the beach in search of the raw materials for her potions, most easily found among the tide-washed rocks. My recommendation as soon as her back was turned was that we should slip quietly away to the privacy of the grand room. This was dismissed out of hand with a touch of the Marchesina's holiday feudal manner. 'What are you suggesting? An hour? Two hours? How plebeian. Everything has its time and place.' This, it was clear, was to be a classic Sicilian performance reserved for the night.

She proposed to cram the maximum of activity into the

daylight hours, and was beginning to knock a hole in my theory that the superabundant energy of my American friends was the product of their vast intake of carefully chosen foods. As far as I could gather, the Marchesina lived on plants grubbed by the Seaweed Eater out of hedgerows supplemented by rare windfalls of offal, of udders, snouts, sacs, valves, ducts, gullets, scrotums, and fish with flat, sucking mouths of the kind that feed largely on sewage. 'Naturally enough,' as she admitted, 'you line up for guts, but I go myself and mention my Angevin ancestry and they put me at the head of the queue.' The Steins would hardly have believed that both the quality and quantity of her diet was adequate to sustain life, but there was no doubt about her intense hyperactivity and I promised myself to bring the matter up with them should we chance to meet again.

The Marchesina had an urge to do strange things such as paddling, and we sloshed about in a few inches of sleazy water with a drifting addition of refuse tossed into the waves by fishermen who cleaned up their catch in boats anchored a short distance off-shore. Next, although she possessed no driving licence – claiming that the necessity to do so was waived in the case of titled persons under Italian law – she demanded to drive the Bianchi and we roared zig-zagging along the sea-front and scattered the children, dogs, cats, chickens and pigs in the high-walled lanes at the back of the town, our speed kept in check only by the fact that the Marchesina did not understand gear-boxes, which restricted us to bottom gear. We inspected the angel's footprint left in black tufa, finding it to be roughly thirteen inches in length, and possessing six toes. There was a garishly painted shack at the end of the beach crowded with visitors, some of whom, said the Marchesina, sat there all day, chewing their way through innumerable helpings of crabs. She had been determined to join them, just for the experience of a single helping. The place was famous, and the result to be expected from its crabs extraordinary. When we arrived we found there was not a table to be had, and not even a mention of the Angevins could procure one. All the customers in sight, chewing away doggedly, looked miserable; beset by the terrible despair of satiety. Frustrated thus, the Marchesina suggested a swim in the nude, but I pointed out that whatever her feudal status nothing in such a case would prevent her mass rape by the crew of the first fishing boat that happened to pass. We settled instead for an exploration of a Greek site just outside the town where the stumps of columns and blunted capitals still littered the ground. She was determined to start digging on the spot, and ordered me to drive back to the hotel where we borrowed a shovel, and within a matter of minutes she had half uncovered a slab of marble with a Greek inscription. This she decided to purloin, but finding that it was too heavy for us to shift, let alone carry off, announced that the theft would have to be postponed until the Seaweed Eater could be brought in to apply her muscles to the task.

One of our problems had been to keep the Seaweed Eater occupied. Like some children, her initial enthusiasm for any project quickly faltered, and she frequently re-appeared to complain to the Marchesina that she was bored.

'Half the time I can't even make out what she's saying,' I said. 'Are you sure she's right in the head?'

'She suffers from a slight impediment, that's all. As for being right in the head, she's as bright as any of us, but in a different way. Please don't look at her in that unpleasant fashion, or she's liable to slip something into your food.'

'How did she come by the name?'

'It's a bit of a joke. Her belly suddenly blew up when she

was 53 and the doctor assumed she was pregnant. "How on earth did you manage it?" he asked her, and she told him it was through eating seaweed.'

'And what happened to the child?'

'There wasn't one. Only a lot of water.'

'But was she sexually active at the time?'

'Exceedingly so,' the Marchesina said. 'And still is.'

We got rid of her by persuading a boatman to take her out hooking octopuses from the shallows. 'That should keep her amused for an hour or two,' the Marchesina said. 'I wonder if she'll manage to seduce him?' The man looked at least seventy, but she assured me that everything was possible in one of these coastal communities where people led bracing lives.

The hotel's garden had been spared the ugly and foolish restoration that the old house – as it had once been – had suffered. We sat in a vine arbour under great, bland inflated gourds shaped like ancient drinking vessels of the simple kind, possessing a symmetry so perfect that it was hard to believe that they were not imitations produced by meticulous craftsmen. Just as distance had conferred a fraudulent dignity on the square of Montelepre, here it had transformed the over-elaborate and over-painted absurdity of the villas of the rich into a charming seaside fantasy. With the coming of evening the pale, glittering sea had drawn in all the colour from the sky and now lay purple and inert beyond a hard frontier of sand. A flock of small white goats, furred like angora rabbits, moved up the beach, darting here and there to forage among the wrack left by the tide. Down by the shack a man was emptying the remains of a hundred crab lunches on the shore, having first hooted several times on a conch shell to attract the birds.

The Marchesina, calmed by the view and perhaps by the

79

hour, had become reflective. 'My father used to come here,' she said. 'I expect you've heard of him.'

'You told me about him yourself.'

'This place used to be full of whores. The great speciality was Roman-style orgies. Men of his kind go on until they wear themselves out. When there's nothing left, they turn to God. He kept a mistress here, another one in Mondello and another in Palermo.'

'I imagine it would have been expected of him.'

'We knew the rot had set in when he decided to rescue them. He paid for priests to move in and give them two or three hours a day religious instruction and then he left them high and dry.'

Some of this was familiar to me. The Duke of Cova-donga's return to the straight and narrow path had been accompanied by considerable dislocation in the lives of those nearest to him. He had seven estates and the houses that went with them, and did his best to give them away. The Church took anything worth having, but much of the property was too run-down for them to bother with. 'My mother and I used to try to talk him out of it, and all he did was point out the passage in the Bible which says "give all thou hast to the poor, and come follow me".'

'Didn't you say he was mixed up in some way with the separatists?' I asked.

'Yes,' she said. 'For which reason – if they take him seriously – they have nothing to hope for. He was a colonel in the Abyssinian war and he went round telling the troops they should love their enemies.'

'He lived up to his principles.'

'Yes, but he should have got out of the army. Did I ever tell you about my dowry?'

'Only that you didn't have one.'

'In the end we got him to agree to tie up what little was left of the property with entails, so that he could give nothing away but his personal effects. When the nuns of the Blessed Assumption of Palermo asked him for a gift he kept the parings of his nails for a year and sent them that. We found out too late he'd sent them in a golden casket, which the nuns refused to return. It was worth about five million lire. That was the last of my dowry. The separatists can have him.'

The people who came to stay at this hotel were members of the middle class with little or no cash. All the money had drained away into the black market, and those who had made great fortunes out of it despised Marinella, preferring Mondello, near Palermo, where they could spend the equivalent of a serving general's income for a week on a block of ice-cream shaped like the cathedral of Milan, stir gold-leaf into their drinks and attract respectful attention by lighting their cigars with 1000 lire notes.

Marinella, said the Marchesina, was a different kettle of fish. It was quite normal for a family who brought along a nursemaid in black boots and white gloves to pay for their accommodation with the family silver, a piece of jewellery, furs or perhaps one of the eighteenth-century Guido Reni's religious paintings, mass-produced by the hundred in the master's atelier, but still good for a week at half pension, last-year's vintage wine thrown in, and a room with a view of rock-blasting operations at the rear of the hotel.

Hotel-guest custom ruled the lives of visitors to Marinella, however free their spirits might have been to follow the vagaries of inclination in their home environment, and it was very difficult not to slip into this. At 6 p.m. every visitor, the Marchesina and I included, walked the length of the sea front, past the crab-eaters' shacks to the cafés strategi-

81

cally placed at the far end, to spend a half hour over a cup of coffee-substitute or a nauseous and bitter aperitif, in a chair screwed into position so that its occupant was bound to face the sea. By 8.15, the human life-blood of the town, drained away in this manner, had flowed back, and we were at table in the hotel, caught up in an atmosphere of anticipation verging on anxiety as we awaited the serving of the soup. To my relief I found that the hotel's pretensions had come to my rescue. Crabs, Marinella style, said a slip clipped to the menu, were not available in the main sala, but could be consumed by guests wishing to try this famous delicacy in a side-room – to which, incidentally, servants in uniform were automatically banished. This got rid of the Seaweed Eater who jabbered her readiness to eat alone rather than forgo her crabs.

Dinner was immensely protracted and the table only reluctantly abandoned by most guests after the last cockle had been sucked dry of its juices, and the last fragment of crust reverently stowed away in the cheek. After dinner ritual strengthened its grip and everyone played canasta with the exception of the Marchesina and myself and the Seaweed Eater, who complained of suffering from a touch of indigestion as well as, once again, of being bored. The Marchesina had brought building blocks to amuse her with and, inevitably, they began to build a castle together.

'How long is this likely to go on?' I asked in English.

'There's no way of knowing,' the Marchesina said.

'Ask her if she wants to go to bed?'

'I have, and she doesn't. She says she isn't tired yet.'

Almost all drinks served after a meal in such establishments were supposed to contain rare herbs that sharpened the sexual proclivities, and we were automatically served strega (witch) tinctured in theory with Amazonian plants.

After two of them I felt myself nodding off. 'Wouldn't a drink help?' I asked.

'She doesn't touch alcohol.'

Again I had the feeling that the Seaweed Eater knew what we were talking about, and would probably have followed the gist of our conversation equally well had we been speaking Arabic. She blinked at me malevolently. 'Just put up with it,' the Marchesina said. 'She'll drop off sooner or later.' The block building restarted, the Seaweed Eater eagerly, almost greedily, adding block after block to a turret until it toppled, and a gasp of consternation was followed by a raucous giggle.

I sat studying the Marchesina's profile; a spare kind of clear-cut beauty, guarded by centuries of privilege and race-conservation, to which had been added a touch of folly. An enamelled gold earring from Etruria twisted a little to show the small, bearded, mocking face of a forgotten god. How lovely, but how complacent she was. Desire had strengthened with the long separation and with the renewal of the sense of mystery that had been so strong at the time of our first contact. Now once again her body was that of a stranger. I dwelt longingly on thoughts of the adventure that awaited me in the great bed set among its gilt carvings and violent tapestries, and the vast terrain of privacy guaranteed by its sheer size.

The Marchesina built up the walls of her castle, and the Seaweed Eater, guffawing her delight and scrabbling with her meaty hands, pulled them down. All around us upper-class citizens with the faces of stained-glass saints endured with stoicism the martyrdom of canasta. Not a voice was raised, no eye turned in our direction. Unlike scopa, foolish diversion of hopeless men, canasta fostered dignity. Upon what malpractices, I wondered, had the fortunes of Marinella been founded? Were these people's forebears no more than the black marketeers of earlier wars?

Their faces drew together, then separated. Their gestures had become stiff and hieratic, expressing adoration or penitence. My eyelids fluttered. They closed on the Seaweed Eater and her jabber, and on all the components, human or otherwise, of this scene. When I opened them again the Marchesina stood over me, a finger on her lips. 'She's asleep,' she said. 'We can go.'

8

THE USUAL COLLECTION of newspapers awaited me at the office. About a dozen of these were delivered every afternoon, made up in the small hours by two men who would then rush out with their copy and wait their turn at the shared printing press. All the news worth printing in Palma was supplied by the happenings of the night, and if the crop happened to be poor the newsmen filled their space with invention. Such manufactured news was instantly recognized by old hands such as myself, and probably by the majority of readers, trained by habit to pass over the obvious absurdities, the space-filling miracles, the visions, the multiple births, the lost children suckled by wild animals, the Italian soldier discovered after ten years' wandering in the mountains of Abyssinia who had lost the power of speech, and pass on quickly to the uncontestable facts, which were often dramatic enough in their own right.

This day the news was of what seemed to be concerted attacks, using explosives, on trade union headquarters in widely separated areas all over the country; in the course of these a number of trade unionists had died. I spent a half-hour with a large-scale map verifying the existence of these places, then came upon a note from Moscato I had over-looked asking me to call.

I went over to the museum and found him going through the week's crop of funerary objects offered at knock-down prices by local grave-robbers working in the Greek necro-polis, amounting to no more than a boring collection of odds and ends left by earlier looters. The only things worth having were the wonderful fakes the robbers tried to pass off as stolen – they were made by the fishermen in their winter quiet season and were so much better, he thought, than the work of the Greek potters of old.

'You were asking me about the miners' strike,' he said. 'I've some news for you. They're going back.'

'I haven't seen anything in the papers about it,' I said.

'There's a news blackout,' he said. 'You won't see any-thing.'

'But why should that be?'

'Because it doesn't suit the owners. Like me they're all separatists for the moment.'

'How did you come to hear about this?'

'I know the engineer at the Siculi mine. They rounded up the ring-leaders and got rid of them.'

'Got rid of them?'

'Down a crevice on one of the old workings. The usual thing. From the company's point of view it's a reasonable solution. It doesn't leave the evidence lying about. After that it was only a question of starving the miners out. Mind you, we're only talking about the Siculi mine, but at least it's a straw in the wind.'

'All I wonder is how it managed to last so long,' I said.

'For political reasons they weren't in any hurry,' Moscato said. 'The longer the thing was allowed to go on the less likely it was to happen again. It cut down over-production, and put up the price of sulphur. I expect you realize this is a blow to people sharing my political views. It tends to cut the ground from under our feet.'

'I can see that,' I told him.

'This brings me to my friend Miraglia,' Moscato said. 'Well, he's not a friend. Actually he's a friend of a friend, but it's the same thing. I'm worried about him. You probably read about the bombings. He's in the same line of business as those men who got their heads blown off a few days ago.'

'Crispi told me the story,' I said. 'Have you been seeing much of him?'

'Not all that much. I haven't actually kept out of his way, but the problem is our personal philosophies are poles apart. On the other hand he's the friend of a friend and that matters a great deal to me. I have this feeling of responsibility, and a lot of people are getting killed.'

'Mostly northerners, I gather from the press.'

'They're foreigners as far as we are concerned, even if they speak the same language. If they want to stir up trouble, why don't they stay where they are? We've enough trouble of our own. Why should they want to break our balls? I've got no use for this son of a bitch Miraglia, on the other hand it's important to me that he should stay alive. Enrico asked me to go through one of those blood-mingling things with him. They used to do it in my father's time. I told him we didn't go in for that kind of thing any longer. We were doing our best to stop living in the past.'

'Do you see anything I can do to help?'

'No,' he said, 'you can't. I only wanted to talk to somebody about it. This stupid man has started a fight to put up agricultural wages, which is fundamentally absurd. If you pay these people more they'll breed more kids. At the moment they average six kids a family, and all a wage rise will mean is they'll put up the average to ten, and there's not enough of everything to go round anyway. The war turned out badly for us. There were hardly any casualties. The Allies took a million prisoners and then let them go, and now they're all back they're producing kids as fast as they can. Anyone can see that this fellow is running against the tide. If he insists on going on like this, what can he expect?'

'Patience,' I said. I quoted the proverb, '"Stitch by stitch the old woman embroiders the cope." Emigration will solve all your problems when it starts up again. Give it a year and your troubles will be at an end. This island will empty as soon as the great rush to get out starts. Miraglia will probably go back to Milan, and everyone will forget he ever existed.'

'We haven't got a year, not even a month,' Moscato said. 'This is happening now. Somebody's convinced this madman he has to organize a cavalcade in the good old Sicilian style of the days of Garibaldi. A thousand peasants and wild men from the hills are going to ride to a feudal estate to stage a symbolical occupation. They're going there with pruning knives stuck in their belts and sickles tied to their saddles, and they'll take the saints out of the churches and carry them with them. Imagine a thousand hillbillies on horseback and another two thousand women and children trailing along the road after them. We're talking about timid people, real cowards – they're afraid of their own shadows –

but when a thousand of them get on their horses and grab up their sheep-shearing scissors and their old hunting guns, something seems to get into them. If anything goes wrong they'll play football with heads.'

'What estate is this?' I asked.

'The Duke of Covadonga's.'

'The Marchesina's father,' I said. 'What a coincidence. Doesn't he live in Palermo?'

'Yes, but he has an estate down here.'

'In ruins?' I asked.

'More or less. His stewards rob him. The usual story. I expect you've heard about him. He's an honorary member of the Franciscans, composes church organ music, and spends half his life on his knees.'

'And he's tied up with the separatists.'

'He writes the manifestos and looks after the Party's conscience. We could do without him.'

'From what I've heard this man doesn't bother much with property. Can you see that he'd object to a symbolical occupation – or a real one if it comes to that?'

'He wouldn't,' Moscato said, 'but all the others would. He has about ten thousand acres of land growing nothing but thistles, which is no good to him or anybody else. But if he lets people simply march in and take over, where's the thing going to stop? And where are all the other landowners going to look for their labour in future? You have to see the problem from their point of view.'

'When's the exercise planned to take place?'

'On Friday,' Moscato said. 'What I propose to do is write to Enrico to say that I renounce all responsibility for his friend's safety from now on. But I know he won't accept it. He'll say, "Look after him. You'll have to answer to me for anything that happens."'

9

CRISPI WAS FULL OF enthusiasm. 'An anachronism and an absurdity,' he said. 'Something like watching history. There have been twenty-two cavalcades in the past hundred years, and believe me, this is the last of them. Absolutely not to be missed.'

We were outside the Hotel Roma. All the preparations had been made and the plate glass windows of the three clubs were boarded over. It was seven in the morning, and so far nothing had happened. 'The thing is,' I said, 'will it have an effect?'

'Of course not, none.'

'Why not?'

'Because this is Sicily. We're all of us feudalists whether

we know it or not. Not even the riders really want to take away the feud, even if they pretend to. Just watch what happens. They'll let off a little steam and then go home, and things will go on as before. They can't imagine any life other than the one they live.'

'Does Miraglia realize this?'

'No, he doesn't. He might as well be a Frenchman, or a German. He has a different kind of mind.'

'He's wasting his time.'

'Yes.'

He passed over a sheet of paper ornamented with his small meticulous handwriting. 'As this in theory is all about the Covadonga estate I thought you might like to know something about the family.'

'You've gone to a lot of trouble,' I said.

'Not at all, I enjoy research. In any case it only took a half hour. It was an excuse to go to the library. Anything to get out of the house.'

I picked up the sheet and began to read.

The Covadonga Family
(as requested)

Duke No. 1: Alonso di Covadonga, Flores Atocha y Caceres. B. 1532. Gentleman adventurer in the suite of the Spanish Viceroy, Medinacelli. Married Sicilian heiress and bestowed her dowry of 150,000 scudi upon the church, following which Archbishop Cabeza, his patron, secured for him his dukedom. Covadonga fell from favour following a 'divine accident' when his ship leading a maritime procession in honour of the Virgin of the Sea capsized in the Bay of Palermo, drowning half the nobility of the City.

Duke No. 3: Roderigo Bivar di Covadonga. B. 1580.

Provided fresh support for the growing theory that religious mania could be hereditary. While soldiering in the Low Countries a Flemish Lutheran read to him a passage from his Bible, omitted in the version authorized in Spain. 'Sell what thou hast. Give the money to the poor, and come follow me.' On his return to Palermo the Duke attempted to comply with the adjuration, was found guilty by the Inquisition of perversion of the natural order, chained to two sodomists, and flung from the roof of the Palace of Justice. In deference to his rank he was caught in a net spread below. The sodomists were strangled on the spot, and the Duke, having been solemnly entreated to renounce his heresy, was released.

Duke No. 7: Cosimo di Covadonga. B. 1692. Dissipated his estates in gifts to religious foundations. In an endeavour to raise cash for more pious donations he obtained fraudulent possession of the Great Seal of the Kingdom, using this to raise important loans in the name of the Spanish nation from the bankers of Florence, none of which were ever repaid. He was ordered to be dressed in a penitent's shift, and exposed to public ignominy.

Duke No. 11: Michele Arcangelo di Covadonga. B. 1811. Believed that God had punished his transgressions by changing him into an hermaphrodite. He was conducted on his own request to Madrid, and there exhibited to the court. His Spanish Majesty was shown a painting of him made while unclothed in childhood, after which, inspecting him through a pane of stained glass, he agreed that this was probably the case.

Duke No 15: Maurizio Giovanni San-Sepuchro di Covadonga. B. 1882. Please judge for yourself. Of this man, the less said the better.

Finally I am of the opinion that it is absurd to believe that religious mania can be genetically endowed, and my contention is fully supported by the views held by our mutual friend Dottore Erminio Moscato.

'From what it says here, we seem to have caught the Marchesina out,' I said. 'She claims descent from the Angevins.'

'Would you expect anything else?' he said.

I was running through the information for a second time when the first of the riders came into the Square, and some of them looked extraordinary enough. Despite the heat of the day to come, they had dressed themselves in mountain-style sheepskins and woollen capes, and many were festooned with protective coral and pagan amulets, and had cows' horns slung round their necks against the evil eye. The horses were of all shapes and sizes, some of them with weird, primitive-looking heads like the survivors of Asian proto-horses sometimes on view in a zoo. Between them they demonstrated every equine effect from dropped backs to bald patches and extensive galls, and seemed universally to suffer from looseness of the bowels, as a result of which, as more and more horsemen arrived, the Square was aslush with ordure. Despite police prohibitions many riders carried billhooks which they brandished furiously as they laughed and screamed at each other. There were hawk-faced men in turbans, with knee-length skirts over their trousers, a woman on horseback who banged endlessly on a tambourine, four men riding abreast who held a red and yellow standard of the old Bourbon kingdom, followed by an image of St Ignazio, patron of convicts and fugitives from justice, brandishing the bloody tongue the executioner had just ripped out.

Above all, there were hundreds of women and swarms of

children carrying dead and dying chickens, the flayed heads of sheep dangling from cords through their eye-sockets, calves-feet, oxtails and tripes, bundles of drooping green-stuff, firewood, and pots and pans of all shapes and sizes.

'These people have come for a festa,' Crispi said. 'Half of them don't know what politics are about. They've just about heard of Christ's birth. Ask them where Italy is and three out of four wouldn't be able to tell you. This isn't a protest, they're here for the ride and a good time.'

Crispi was afraid of horses and the youngest riders, boys in their teens, were charging round the Square to show off. He tipped up a table and used it as a barricade.

'I've just seen a man I gave a helping hand with his legal problems,' Crispi said. 'He asked me what they meant by symbolical occupation. "Does that mean we keep the land, or doesn't it? What's the point of going just to look at it?" I had to agree that there wasn't much point. "Look at it this way," I told him. "You'll get a day off work. Everybody will have a picnic. Make a nice change for the family." "That's about it," he said. "It'll be a nice break, just as long as the Duke doesn't get angry, and call in the police."' The rumour had been going round, Crispi said, that the real reason they were going up to the casa padronale on the estate was to pay their respects to the Duke on the occasion of his sixty-fifth birthday, and some of the women were taking a half kilo of ricotta, and a few eggs twisted in a cloth with paper charms and birthday messages. 'We laugh at them,' Crispi said, 'but crowds can be funny things. They panic for no reason at all, and sometimes they turn nasty. You can never tell. A thousand men on horseback are something to be reckoned with. Believe me, the police will be keeping out of sight.'

There was an outburst of cheering in the crowd and Miraglia came into view. I'd seen him several times before, but at a distance, a small ineffectual-looking man, the reverse of a firebrand in his appearance. He was well into middle-age and old for his years, with a straggling grey beard, and dressed when I'd seen him like a clerk, in an atrociously-fitting navy-blue suit. At this moment he was mounted on one of the smallest and ugliest horses I'd ever seen, and looking uncomfortable, and I remembered Moscato saying that he'd never ridden a horse before, and had had to take lessons for this occasion.

At this point Crispi's movements became furtive. He had hunched himself up in his chair, and a hag-ridden expression had screwed up his face. 'Don't look,' he whispered, 'but I'm being spied upon.' He shielded his face with a faded and illegible menu, upon which a sparrow had recently defecated. I was surprised because the attendance of the locals at this hour of the morning was sparse. A few yards away a man sat with a black hat pulled down over his eyes, but all Sicilians look like conspirators, so there was nothing special about this. 'It's the widow,' Crispi said. 'She suspects I'm engaged to be married, and she's having me watched. She keeps a tag on my movements, and when I get home at nights she checks up on where I've been.' He fidgeted in an agonized way, then jumped up. 'Sorry, she's been dosing me up with something that keeps me on the run. Keep my seat, I'll see you in a moment.' He dashed into the Roma, and I waited ten minutes or more for him, but he didn't come back.

By now the cavalcade was on the move and the Square was emptying. As soon as I could get to my car parked in one of the back streets, I drove out along a farm track that joined the main road to the Covadonga estate-house about three miles out of town, and there from the summit of a low hill after an hour's wait I watched the approach of the cavalcade. This landscape was of the real stuff of feudal land. Nobody had cultivated it for decades, perhaps a century, and a prairie of majestic thistles stretched almost to the horizon in all directions. Through it moved the soft yellow snaking of dust raised by four thousand hooves, although from this point of vantage nothing showed of the horsemen but a few banners poking up through the dust. Three miles further down the road, the walls and battlements of the estate-house of Covadonga showed above the sea of blue-grey vegetation. In about 1860 the peasants had burned down the original building, and the 13th Duke being away on pilgrimage, only the caretaker, his wife, children and various domestic animals that happened to be about had had their throats cut by the great-great-grandfathers of the present demonstrators. The house's medieval appearance was due to the fact that on his return the Duke had rebuilt it in Scottish baronial style, importing Highland cattle to improve the view from its windows – all of which animals had died from heatstroke shortly after their arrival.

The daunting, almost overpowering presence everywhere of thistles contributed to the deflection of the cavalcade from the original plan of action, which – as explained by Miraglia to his followers – was to carry out a dignified and peaceful advance on the estate-house, and there, having made due and formal notice of its intention, set about a symbolical and propagandist clearing and cultivation of a patch of unutilized land. Now – as I was later to learn – halfway to the Duke's baronial folly, a crisis arose between two factions: a wholly non-violent party led by Miraglia who were determined to stick strictly to the plan, and a splinter group of younger and more impatient men who raised an outcry in favour of action without the speech-making, there and then.

It was the thistles in their ancient role as guardians and tenants of feudal land that set off the explosion. Finding themselves free through the landlord's neglect to wander and colonize, they had spread unchecked from fields into roads, overwhelming the ruins of ancient villages, forming thickets that made the going hard even for horsemen, let alone the footsore followers of all ages that straggled painfully after them. The wailing of tired and hungry children went up, and the break-away faction, who had had enough of Miraglia's orders, called a halt and started to clear an open space where the families coming up from behind could rest and cook their food. Miraglia, trotting round on his pigmy horse to urge the men on in his small, high-pitched voice, was ignored. The men charged into the thistles, cutting and slashing out in all directions, chopping them down, beheading them, and kicking the sliced-up fragments of the plants about just as they would have dealt with the bodies of their massacred human oppressors in the old days.

In a short time they had cleared an acre of thistles, rendering themselves liable in doing so to a law still on the statute book which forbade interference of any kind with feudal lands under penalty of 'lesser mutilation' – the loss of a thumb. By this time many of them were depleted both of energy and wrath, and those who had made it clear that they were determined to stay settled to light fires, open the wine, feed the thistle-tops to the horses, and put the cooking pots on to the boil. Miraglia attempted another reproachful harangue, which no one listened to, then gave up, and gathering together some thirty or so of his hard-core followers, rode off towards the estate-house.

Having nothing better to do I strolled down to join the backsliders. By this time they had put behind them all thought of political protest, and settled to enjoy themselves

97

in traditional fashion, horses hobbled and roped together, cooking pots bubbling out the aroma of stewing offal, the men puffing obligatory holiday cheroots, the children making nuisances of themselves in any way they could. Sicilians love to include perfect strangers in their parties, so I was received as a member of this huge and instantly formed extended family. Seven journalists had gone along with the cavalcade and were interviewing the riders and putting absurd stories into their mouths as well as inventing imaginary adventures for inclusion in their pieces. We tasted and praised all the various messes, some palatable, and some verging on the horrific. The wine pressed on us was thick, sweet and full of sediment. Its instant effect on the peasants confirmed the theory that drunkenness often results from a determination to get drunk and is to be achieved with a minimal alcoholic intake.

This general befuddlement may have been at the bottom of a dangerous episode following shortly after. A woman who had gone off into the uncleared thistles, probably to relieve herself, suddenly shrieked 'police' and the cry was taken up. A number of men were running about in an excited fashion; there was a good deal of shouting, then a rush towards the perimeter of the cleared space which carried me along with it. Nobody seemed quite to know what was happening. Men were pointing and shouting, waving their fists and throwing stones, and nobody stopped to explain what all the fury was about. Finally I picked out the figure of a carabiniere standing as still as a scarecrow among the tall thistles, wonderfully camouflaged by the grey–blue of his uniform which exactly matched the colour of the plants. Having sighted one policeman I knew what to look for, and soon spotted three more, the nearest being about a hundred yards away.

The shouting of insults and the stone-throwing went on, and since the carabinieri seemed in no mood to do anything to stop it, more and more demonstrators joined in and the boldest of them, including a few women, made a threatening advance into the thistles determined to give themselves the satisfaction of seeing the police break and run. It was later revealed that the town's full complement of seven carabinieri had been committed to this action with the nominal and highly reluctant support of five plainclothes agents of the Pubblica Sicurezza under the command of a doctor of law who had joined the police only the previous week.

At this point I thought it prudent to withdraw to the vantage point where I had left the car, and there I watched the confused events that followed through my binoculars. In my experience one tends to indulge in small personal deceptions and over-dramatize situations of this kind. If I had been asked at that moment to give a snap figure of the number of men attacking the police, I should have said a hundred or more, but it turned out that there were thirty-nine. Similarly, when the shooting started my imagination staged a battle. It began with the distant, hollow cough of a large-bore hunting gun; then followed a number of pinging rifle-shots – volleys as I assured myself. Later I discovered that most of these were fired into the air as a deterrent rather than to inflict damage. The action was restricted to a small area where peasants were charging through the thistles towards the police who seemed to be in retreat, although keeping up a few sporadic shots. This was no more than a small agitated corner in a stubbornly pacific landscape with larks leaping high into the air to rattle their song against the popping of musketry fire before falling back, and a few hump-backed clouds the shape of turtles creeping across the sky.

The police disappeared into the distance, blotted up in the battle-grey camouflage of the estate, the attacking peasants slowed their advance, stopped, then began to trickle back. Closer at hand the women and camp-followers of various descriptions were packing away the impedimenta of their picnics, and loading up hand carts. A number of riders were already in the saddle and had turned back towards the town. This part of the cavalcade, accounting for ninety per cent of those who had joined in, was clearly at an end. The encounter, as I was to learn later that day, had been far from bloody. Three carabinieri had been struck by flying stones, although able to keep going. A fourth had had to have a fragment of a nail from a home-made cartridge removed from his cheek. Of the demonstrators, only one had been wounded – a woman who had suffered a flesh wound from a spent bullet in the thigh. A horse was the only other casualty, being caught by a ricochet in the neck, and stitched up satisfactorily on the spot.

An account was given me by Crispi of the meeting at the estate-house between Miraglia and the Duke – received by him from a relative who had failed at law and was obliged now to work as a day labourer.

'Let's face it,' Crispi said. 'They were scared. Francisco said he couldn't stop trembling, but knew he had to go through with it. He couldn't get rid of the feeling that what they were doing was in some way despicable. A kind of betrayal. It was something that seemed to go against nature. The closer they got to the estate-house the slower they went. Even Miraglia seemed to hang back, and when they got there he gave me the impression of being undecided what to do. In the end he got off his horse and went and knocked at the gate. The Duke must have been waiting for them because he came out immediately.'

Crispi made a disparaging face – like many professional men he was strongly anticlerical. 'He was got up to look like a monk. Just as I'd imagined he would be. There was a chaplain with him with a platterful of communion bread. The Duke went round kissing them all and the chaplain handed out the bread. Naturally they had to cross themselves before putting it in their mouths. All this religious paraphernalia caught them off their guard.'

'I can imagine the scene,' I said.

'They were there to protest,' Crispi said. 'But what against? God? Only our rulers are atheists. Remember this man is very clever, and he couldn't have been more pleasant. He addressed everybody as "my brother". Nauseating to you and me, but effective with peasants. The chaplain quoted from the Sermon on the Mount. "Blessed are the meek."'

'It was all a waste of time, then?'

'Worse than that in a way. The Duke said, "Take what you want, it's all yours." What were they to do? That wasn't what they'd come for, and he knew it. He called Miraglia's bluff. All they'd keyed themselves up for was a symbolical occupation, and the Duke said that a symbolical one was better than none at all, and he'd help them with it. He had a garden at the estate-house with fruit trees and flower beds, and he said, "My brothers, let us join forces to put an end to this frivolity." So they cut all the trees down and dug up the flower beds. The Duke told them he couldn't think of a more symbolical act than the one they'd just done. He was laughing at them.'

'So what's to happen?'

'In my opinion nothing,' Crispi said. 'The estate's no good to anyone in any case. They would have to bring in

101

water to grow anything more than beans and winter wheat, and where would the capital come from? The main thing is the fuss is over and done with. Miraglia made a mistake to encourage people to risk their lives and liberty for something that's not worth fighting for. Better to tell them to do the best they can with what they have. That way nobody gets killed.'

10

THERE WERE STRONG differences of opinion in Palma di Cava as to the effectiveness, impact, even the purpose of the Cavalcade and no one seemed quite sure what had happened. Such members of the downtrodden masses who retained any ability to think saw it as a small and hesitant step along the ill-paved road to social justice. The man in the street – if one existed – objected to the way it had held up traffic. Members of the Civilized People's Club regarded it as a conspiracy against the nation, sometimes adding 'but it got them nowhere'. Newspaper coverage was equally undecided. The *Corriere* spoke of a massacre narrowly averted in an eye-witness report secured by their man under a hail of bullets. *Il Messagero* had unearthed a plot to take over

Palma, hatched somewhere in the East. *Voce*, with a circulation predominantly among churchgoers, and specializing in scientific investigation of the supernatural, concentrated on the conflicting news story of the day, which occupied its front page:

Excitement was caused in Palma today by the appearance to Ugo Bosco, 41, shoemaker, Vico Vasco 13, of the Archangel Michael in the Parco Margarita. Bosco was endeavouring to extract a bee sting from his toe when a stranger, dressed as a foreign tourist in hiking garments, approached him with gestures of sympathy. The stranger touched the inflamed spot causing the instant departure of the pain. He then smiled and turned away, whereupon Bosco noticed wings somewhat larger than those of a goose protruding from an aperture in his shirt. The incident, witnessed by several persons in the vicinity, has been reported to the appropriate office of the Vicariate of Palermo, for registration as a miraculous happening.

Later in the day Moscato phoned. 'How would you like to meet the great man? He's here now. I'm doing my best to make him go back to Milan, and leave us in peace. I've told him. "They've had enough of you. You've outstayed your welcome. Why don't you go now while you're all in one piece?"'

I went over to the museum and found the doctor with Miraglia crowded among the overflow of exhibits, drinking the museum's pickling spirit in which a variety of berries had been steeped. 'This encourages you to speak your mind,' Moscato said.

Miraglia seemed to have put on weight but was nevertheless in some way shrivelled. He had a bad skin condition with a rash on his forehead which he rubbed continually with the back of his hand, and stomach trouble causing him to leave the room more than once to fart as quietly as possible on the other side of the door. Miraglia still looked very much of an outsider – someone Sicilians would never wholly accept.

Moscato said, 'He's come here whining for advice. The roof in the trade union place has fallen in. They're drawing nasty signs on his front door, and someone has cut his cat's tail off. What does he expect?' To Miraglia he said, 'I can't understand why Enrico ever let you out of his sight.'

I could see that Miraglia was determined that nothing should put him out. The story was that he had become an addict of the card game scopa, in which players never cease to revile each other, and this had taught him how to receive and return insults. 'This is an old friend from England,' Moscato said, referring to me. 'I don't know what he's supposed to be doing here, and he probably doesn't himself, but an outsider's view might be of some use. You'll probably pay more attention to him than me.'

'It's these chalk marks on the door,' Miraglia said. 'What are they supposed to signify? The roof doesn't bother me, it was in bad shape, but I'd like your opinion on the mysterious signs. Also, why should anyone want to damage my cat?'

Moscato was staring at him with real or pretended disdain. Miraglia was a man who fiddled with any object within reach – in this case a small stone dog somebody had dug up in the ruins of Segesta – and it was hard not to find some resemblance in the time-smoothed pug features, which were at once impudent and ingratiating, to those of the man from Milan. 'Is there anything I should do about it?' Miraglia asked.

'It's really of not much importance whatever you do,' Moscato said. 'Someone wants you to go. It's a way of dropping a hint. I'd take it if I were you.'

'Does this suggest to you that I've made enemies?'

'That,' said Moscato, 'is exactly what it suggests. Besides falling flat on its face that cavalcade of yours upset people. All you did was to shut down the shops for a day and fill the square with horse-shit.'

'I wouldn't expect you to understand,' Miraglia said. 'It was a trial of strength that succeeded, and it raised the level of political consciousness.'

'Which will promptly fall again,' Moscato said.

'People have been forced to sit up and take notice.'

'But all they're talking about is the way you let the Duke twist you round his little finger.'

'Any man can experience a change of heart,' Miraglia said. He grinned widely, the deep lines round his mouth emphasized by the stubble left by a bad shave. 'The Duke has seen the light.'

'I'm sorry, but you're a fool,' Moscato told him.

'And you're a reactionary. A figure from the past. Why don't you pluck up courage, cut your ties with the feudalists and join us?'

'I want to be there when you sow your beans in the Duke's garden. Let's face it, my friend, compared to Covadonga you're an infant in arms.'

'The Duke is a highly intelligent man who realizes that feudalism is dead and done with. He's decided to move with the times before it's too late.'

'To the extent of giving his land away?'

'Yes.'

'The only land you'll get from the Duke is enough to bury yourself in. What is dead and done with is this cavalcade

106

nonsense. Now let's talk about your personal predicament. You seem to have no idea of what you're up against. Somebody chalks crosses and setting suns all over your door, and somebody else chops your cat's tail off. Haven't you any idea what comes next?'

'No, but I can follow the drift of the discussion.'

'I used to be assistant coroner here. A lot of people in Palma fall downstairs, or they may even have the bad luck to eat the wrong kind of mushrooms, or drink disinfectant out of a cough mixture bottle, or get themselves run over by a passing car that goes out of control. Whatever it is, the inquest takes five minutes, and the certificate says death from misadventure. Be warned in time. A week or two ago you were surrounded by your friends. Now they're gone. Ask yourself why? Because you're seen as a bad risk. Mussolini used to say better a day as a lion than a hundred years as a sheep. Do you agree with that?'

'No more than he did.'

'And you want to live a little longer?'

'There's a lot to be done.'

'Very well, then. Since I can't drive you away, here are two things to bear in mind. First of all, who cooks for you?'

'Nobody. I go out for a snack.'

'Don't. If the woman you lodge with won't cook you a meal, make yourself sandwiches. Much more important still, never be alone.'

'I never am.'

'But you are at night.'

'Well yes, at the moment I am.'

'Do something about it,' Moscato said. 'Make your landlady a happy woman. After ten o'clock lock the door, get into bed with her, and stay there, or it won't be long before I have to write Enrico a letter with bad news.'

11

A CHANGE IN THE mood, a slowing down, a loss of the sense of urgency was linked to lethargy of the season as the full weight of midsummer fell upon the town. People looked at the date on the calendar and decided they couldn't be bothered to put themselves out about anything. Those who could afford to take it easy put themselves under doctor's orders to spend at least three hours sleeping off the midday meal, and to ration themselves to walks of not more than one hundred paces, slowly taken, in the shade. The great church of St Maria della Vittoria was filled all day with the devout who dozed comfortably between prayers.

Reprisals against malcontents of all descriptions were in full swing. As the ability of the provisional government and its supporters to stifle protest had a bearing on the success and future of the separatist movement it was part of my job to observe and report on these happenings. In the case of the mines where the ex-strikers who'd gone back were certainly paying for their mistake there was nothing whatever to be done, as not even the most assiduous and enterprising newspaper reporter could worm his way into one. Retaliation against peasants who had taken part in the cavalcade was conducted quite openly, and it seemed that the landowners had decided that in their case the most effective course was to do their best to see to it that none of those who took part should ever be employed again.

Day labourers offered themselves for hire at three a.m. on six days of the week in the cattle market in the Piazza Mazzini. This was a medieval spectacle I'd often been urged to witness, but managed to avoid until some days after the cavalcade, when most reluctantly I set my alarm for two-thirty and took myself over there. The piazza, which I saw for the first time, was in the semi-derelict outskirts of the town; an unpaved space ringed with collapsed buildings and featuring a stockade lit by acetylene lamps suspended from poles. I was late in arriving, but by this time, half-past-three, sixty or seventy men had gathered who were offering their services for that day. A few estate-foremen were going round, feeling their muscles, and conducting little private auctions encouraging them to bid against each other to force down the going price of 250 lire for ten hours' work. There was some false joviality in the air; the estate-foremen laughed a lot, and went in for a good deal of back-slapping, and their victims did their best to manage a little weak laughter in return. There was no light work, such as vine-pruning or hoeing, on offer that day, it had been announced. Anyone taken on would be set to work terrace-building: labour of a back-breaking and dangerous kind since the gradients were so steep that the worst of them were virtually cliffs, and because of landslides, pullers-up with safety ropes were employed.

Soon after my arrival the word went round that there were four times the number of applicants for the jobs that were going, so it was decided to arrange an elimination contest known as *u mulo sciancatu* (the lame mule). About thirty men were lined up, and packs filled with earth and stones were strapped to their shoulders for a race across the square. Several collapsed and gave up, and the first eight across the finishing line were pushed aside and formed into a separate group where they waited in expectation of being taken on.

At this point the blow fell, the plan clearly having been to raise hopes before dashing them to the ground. Each man was asked to state whether or not he had been in the cavalcade, and those who admitted that they had were told that there was no work for them and they need not apply again. Another lame mule race followed and once again ex-cavalcade participants who had finished well up in the field found themselves excluded. Not only that, but the news spread that in future all applicants would have to be in possession of certificates of good conduct. These would be issued after investigation of their background by the police office or that of the Archpriest of Palma. It was rumoured that when emigration to the States – upon which so many hopes were fixed – was renewed, the possession of such certificates would be required.

I happened to recognize one of the foremen I'd known of old, a reasonable fellow called Di Stefano, who'd started as a day labourer, been involved in a bad accident but kept on through the intervention of Minasola. He looked on his last legs and when I went over to make myself known he burst into a fit of coughing. They'd just unstrapped the pack from a man's back and pulled him to his feet. 'This is what we call the survival of the fittest,' Di Stefano said. Next day Moscato mentioned that this man had TB, and they'd given him six months to live.

'Isn't the lame mule illegal?' I asked.

'It was, but it isn't any more. This is a democracy now, which means that people are entitled to do what they like.'

'I'm all in sympathy with them,' Di Stefano said, 'but I suppose they asked for it. They tried on a blackmail. It didn't come off, and this was all they could expect.'

Later that day I ran into Miraglia, of all places at the house of a consultant engineer employed by the Siculi mine, where an after-birth burying ceremony was taking place. Miraglia was there with a friend from Milan who was writing a book on Sicilian customs, and although the engineer certainly knew of his reputation as a dangerous agitator he couldn't have been pleasanter or more helpful. The wife had given birth in the morning and in the afternoon the placenta was ceremonially interred. Dr Moscato had arranged this experience for me, and in addition to Miraglia and his friend, three of the engineer's colleagues were present. Champagne was served, then a priest led the way followed by the father holding a small white casket to an area at the bottom of the garden where the interment took place. A boy's placenta is buried somewhere in the open where its influence upon him in later life will encourage him to go forth and seek his fortune in the world. That of a girl, as the father informed us, must be disposed of within the house – most commonly down the lavatory – 'because a woman's place is the home'. 'This is something,' he said, 'from which I divorce myself intellectually. Nevertheless it is pleasant to keep the old customs alive besides being an excellent excuse to have one's friends round for a drink.'

Miraglia was dazzled by the man's civilized attitude. 'He probably detests me,' he said, 'but he was so friendly.' He and his friend were going off to a café at the back of the square to play scopa.

'Why don't you join us?' he asked.

'I'll watch you,' I said.

They made a start with the game Miraglia explained to his friend Bonelli as being a great Sicilian institution, and Bonelli took occasional notes. He wore the kind of small, perky hat with a feather stuck in it that Miraglia had worn when he arrived from Milan, and there was something about his movements and his bright, alert eye that reminded me of a squirrel.

'I'm explaining to him that he has to let out a yell whenever he loses a trick, and now he's lost one,' Miraglia said. Bonelli dutifully yelled, and several men at neighbouring tables looked up in surprise.

They played a few more hands, then put the cards away. 'And how are things with you after the recent excitement?' I asked Miraglia.

'Well,' he said, 'very well. Whatever Moscato may say I regard our demonstration as having been a great success.'

'Were you able to put the roof in order at your centre?'

'Within a matter of days. Several of our members are carpenters by profession and they offered their services without charge. I never cease to be amazed at the enthusiasm and the generosity of our local friends.'

'And how's the cat?'

'Quite recovered. He looks ridiculous without a tail, but manages very well. My impression is that there may have been some bad blood at the time of the cavalcade but that's a thing of the past. In other words all is forgiven. While we're on the subject, I may as well say that nobody can tell me the Sicilians are as black as they're painted. The image most people have of them is quite false. Take the example of the engineer today – the way he went out of his way to be kind to three absolute strangers. What splendid hospitality.'

'Do they still write signs on your door?' I asked.

'Yes, they do. But they're quite different. My new theory is they're the work of children. Funny little stylized men running about apparently throwing things. The work of a child of about six or seven. Amusing in its way.'

Bonelli broke in. 'I find them quite interesting. They remind me of the rock drawings made by primitive tribes we used to see in Africa.'

'Anyway, you're quite happy with the way things are going?' I said to Miraglia.

'More than happy,' Miraglia said. 'We're gaining new support every day. And I'll let you into a secret. We're setting up a new project. Something that will make the world sit up and take notice. I mustn't say any more at this stage except that we're full of optimism.'

12

THE SARACENS HAD been in Sicily for three centuries, and in summer, with the onset of night, Palma di Cava reverted gracefully to its Arabian past. As the winds lost breath the town filled with a stagnant spiciness. Shortly before sundown a rising indigo mist set the houses afloat, and it was at that hour, sooner or later, that one noticed for the first time that they were all cubes, capped here and there, where there had been a little money in the family in the past, with a shallow cupola or dome.

These were the faded watercolour scenes through which I walked every evening on my way to the Square, a captive to the ritual socializing, often conducted largely in silence, which had become the indispensable climax to the day.

Two days after my meeting with Miraglia at the house of the engineer I left my office at the usual time and set out for the centre. I was immediately struck by the sensation of there being 'something in the air'. This was a town with its own mute, hidden life, its nuances of atmosphere, almost its heartbeat. Perhaps because they had lived for so many centuries in the shadow of the volcano its people had developed a kind of corporate susceptibility to the slightest variation in the rhythm of their existence. They reminded me of dogs, their nerves tuned to the remotest of seismic convulsions, distressed not only by the reality of an earthquake but by the anticipation of one.

On this evening people were behaving not quite as I expected them to, although it was impossible to put a finger upon where the difference lay. There were fewer aimless strollers to be seen in the streets than usual, fewer shutters had been opened to let in the cool evening air. The few scopa players in the bars cursed each other with less spirit. Shortly before reaching the Square I made my usual stop for a thimbleful of coffee substitute at a café frequented by Catanians, the jokers of Sicily, who burst into almost insane laughter on the slightest provocation, composed obscene verse and played silly tricks on each other. This bar was called the Gran Paradiso, because its walls were decorated with lugubrious scenes of the Kingdom of Heaven from which alcohol was debarred. The great evening joke here was to paint the face of one's friends over those of the blessed, huddled together in depressed groups waiting for exit-visas to come through to hell, where liquor was still procurable. The Gran Paradiso was very quiet. All the previous day's faces painted over those of the saints had been blacked out, but no one had so far been inspired to pick up the paint pot and brush kept ready on the counter and set the evening's fun in motion in the usual way.

I left within minutes and walked on to the Square. There, too, things were very quiet. It was the first time in my experience that the window seats offering a ringside view of life from the Civilized People's Club, the Cultural Circle and the Association of ex-Combatants had not been taken, and not only that, but there were empty tables outside the Roma where casuals like myself, who had not quite achieved the status of regulars, were accommodated in the normal way only as a favour by the old head waiter, Giovanni. A dozen or so customers were seated in my immediate vicinity, but it appeared that no one had been served. They seemed restless and a little nervous, like passengers on a railway station with their eyes on the clock ready to grab their luggage and make a rush for the train.

Old Giovanni made a brief and indecisive appearance in the doorway behind us before something he saw drove him from view. This was a man wearing a tartan cap and plaid trousers who had dropped into a chair at a table a few yards from where I sat, to discuss some matter, notebook in hand, with two of the regulars. After a while he got up, left them and came towards me. I recognized him as Inspector Volpe, of the Pubblica Sicurezza, whom I knew slightly, an old career policeman now pushed into the background by an academic with friends in the Ministry of Justice.

The Inspector, who – although he was far from affluent – suffered from a local form of melancholia known as 'the sadness of the rich', sat down and opened his notebook. 'Good evening, Doctor,' I said. Only chief inspectors were entitled to be addressed as doctor, but I knew that it was a courtesy he would appreciate. A uniformed policeman had appeared in the background to head off several customers of the Roma who had hastily left their seats. Through the window of the

Civilized People another policeman drifted into sight, herding the members like sheep, and now I understood why attendance at the clubs had suddenly fallen off.

'I'm afraid this is a bother, Mr Philips,' the Inspector said. 'Could I ask you to describe to me anything unusual that may have come to your notice since you've been seated at this table?'

'I've seen nothing in any way unusual at all, Doctor. Rather less customers than I expected to find, but nothing more than that.'

It was instantly clear to me that someone had been killed, probably shortly before my arrival, and Volpe and his men would now be compelled to question everyone found in a public place in the area. 'What did you see? What did you hear?' – a barren exercise for the answer would always be the same: 'I saw nothing, I heard nothing.' A foreigner taken in this net could waste a little energy by over-conscientiously enquiring what all the questioning was about, but it saved time and trouble to get the thing over in the easiest possible way, and no doubt the police, too, were happy with a blank-faced denial.

'I saw nothing,' I said.

'And you heard nothing?'

'Absolutely nothing.'

Every policeman in the town had been sent here committed to a routine of stultification noting down names, addresses, residence, father and mother's name and whether alive or dead. But nothing would come of it all and next day all the sheets of paper covered with punctilious and pointless detail would go into the waste-paper basket. This was as it had always been, and would always be.

'Please tell me, Mr Philips, how long have you been seated here?' The Inspector was undoubtedly bored but unruffled. He had learned how to disarm frustration and was admired for the urbane façade behind which he concealed the professional ferocity acquired in a life devoted to the repression of crime. He drew on a repertoire of small gestures and actions. When he took out his notebook he tapped it sharply once, opened it then flattened it on the table top with a light blow of the hand. He knitted his brows with a show of perplexity and his yellowed eyes moved sideways in each direction, like those of an Indian dancer. An instant of alertness passed and the rueful smile of normality was reinstated. Almost certainly the Inspector was quite unaware of these slight personal changes that had gone on. 'I've been here five minutes at most, Doctor. I've hardly sat down.'

'I looked in at the Gran Paradiso, and was there for a matter of minutes too.'

'In fact you've been on the move. Of course, I understand. Was the door of the Gran Paradiso open while you were there?'

'It was. The fans never work. It can be quite stuffy.'

'Shots were fired,' the Inspector said. 'Sicilians are often too absorbed in whatever they happen to be doing to pay much attention to such things. With the door open you should have heard.'

'I'm sorry, Doctor. I've been living in Palma off and on for quite a time. Perhaps I've taken to concentration in the Sicilian way. Where did this happen?'

'Very near here.'

'In the Square itself?'

'In the Square.'

'Who was it?'

'I am not in a position to tell you that.'

'Can I see the body?'

118

'You cannot. All persons must continue to remain seated until the preliminary enquiries are completed,' he said. 'After that they may pass the marked-off area where the incident took place, but they must be able to prove if required to do so that they are actually going somewhere. Photographs are not allowed.'

He closed his notebook, rapped it with a knuckle and got up and moved away, his mouth committed forever to its sorrowful smile that was without significance of any kind. Of all the trades practised in Palma di Cava there were few more routine than his. Our encounter had been hardly more than a matter of liturgical formularies. Quite accidentally I had conformed to local standards of conduct in such a situation, presenting myself as blind and deaf in things that did not concern me, and this – if he had any feelings at all on the subject – he had probably accepted with approval.

Two men awaited him at a nearby table where the small sad farce was to be repeated once more. I wanted to call after him. I had an impulse to catch up with him and bombard him with questions: 'Inspector, as an expert in these matters, does it seem a little strange to you that the killings for which your country is celebrated should so often be carried out in well-lit and frequented places like this? Inspector, why do you so often allow the body to remain – placed on display, as it would seem to a stranger – all night? If this man had died of a heart attack he would have been quietly shoved away under the earth within twenty-four hours. Why the hearse drawn by eight horses, and the car following with the piled-up wreaths? Do they ring all the bells in other towns for a murder? This is a tragedy, not a matter for public rejoicing. Is such a death seen in any way as contributing to the welfare of the community? Inspector, do you believe that men killed in this way realize that they are about to die? If not why are they so often freshly shaved and dressed in their best clothes? Do you see, however dimly at the back of your mind, that this present event may have some connection with the shedding of sacrificial blood, with fertility of the soil and the fruitfulness of harvest? Inspector Volpe, what role do you play in this? Do you accept yourself as an accomplice of fate?'

For two hours we sat there; the men in the clubs rearranged in rows as before, facing outwards, contemplating the emptiness of the Square, and the rest of us outside the cafés deserted by the waiters, waiting for something to happen. A little group of men had gathered under the archway, illuminated by an arc-light, at the far end of the Square. The police were there with their tapes and the chalk with which they marked the outline of the body on the pavement or the cobbles upon which it lay. Nothing would be allowed to disrupt the order in which the parts of the drama were assembled. The police surgeon in a car with a revolving blue lamp was next to arrive – followed by the forensic and ballistic experts, each at the wheel of a brand-new baby Fiat. Behind them, when their bloodied gloves had been removed and tossed into separate white pails, came the stampeding photographers, squatting, standing on chairs, hoisted onto each others' shoulders to set off their flashes. Last of all came the ambulance, the driver of which had given a lift to an undertaker in a top hat. At the time of my last experience of an episode of this kind, two years before, professional wailing women had announced at this point the identity of the victim who had been then left (at the opposite end of the Square) until dawn. Since then things had changed for the worse, and there was longer to wait for the name. As the old waiter Giovanni boasted to me a few minutes later, 'We've moved with the times.'

There was a small queue waiting to use the Roma's phone. In the end my turn came. I rang Moscato. 'Someone's been murdered,' I said. 'Have you heard any news?'

'Yes, I have,' he said. 'But I don't feel like talking about it. I've just been on the line to Enrico.'

13

'I HAVE A SOLUTION to our problem,' said the Marchesina, 'and perhaps a nice surprise for you.'

We sat uncomfortably on the narrow stone bench facing the fountain by Volpone, which the Seaweed Eater, in a bad humour, had emphatically declined to activate for my benefit on this occasion. The problem was the barriers set up to love-making by the Marchesina's many aesthetic scruples and inhibitions. In all likelihood she was inventor of the Italian equivalent of vibes – *vibrazioni* – constantly used to reinforce her objections. The palace in its normally desolate state was full of bleak *vibrazioni*, and through some miscalculation in dates the furniture that should have been in place for my visit was not, although the Seaweed Eater had just come in with a single contribution, the model of a samurai in full war-gear, strapped to her back. My suggestion for making the best of this arid situation in whatever way we could was haughtily dismissed. 'You are prone to banality,' she said. After the experience of Ferdinand IV's bed, anti-climax was hard to avoid.

The Marchesina's suggestion was original, even adventurous. The woods at the foot of the volcano concealed many ancient shrines of Venus. She said that she would not find such surroundings banal. 'Of all the occasions in life,' she said, 'this is the one in which style counts for most.' I was struck by foreboding. 'What happens about the Seaweed Eater?' I asked. 'I feel obliged to take her with me; however, I have worked out a plan for keeping her out of our hair.'

Nowadays all the shrines were named after female martyrs, St this, that or the other, who had been put to dreadful deaths, usually by the Romans. Most of them seemed to have been sited to test their visitors' spirit and endurance in locations offering the maximum difficulty of access, such as on the edge of a cliff or across a roaring torrent. The only one to which we could travel most of the way by car was the shrine of Marichiara set in an almost impenetrable wood used by rustlers to hide their stolen cattle. The Seaweed Eater was bundled as usual into the dicky seat of the Bianchi, and we set out for this.

We bumped about ten miles up country roads passing at one point many yellow flowers growing on the banks. 'Dandelions,' the Marchesina said, pointing them out. 'This is the season for them. They're getting rare and are in great demand.' The Seaweed Eater had spotted them too, and we could hear her shrieks of excitement above the rattlings of the car. Soon after this we were in the forest where we left the car and began a scramble through the black and sinister pine grove up to the shrine.

This was a prehistoric construction shaped like a beehive with a low triangular entrance half obscured by ferns, and we were crouching down to climb through it when the Marchesina held up a hand. 'Attention,' she said. 'Watch where you tread. You find snakes in these places in summer.' The Seaweed Eater jumped back gibbering with fear, and the Marchesina said, 'I know this doesn't interest you, why don't you go and collect some dandelions. We'll take a quick look round and follow you down.'

The Seaweed Eater scuttled off. 'Once she starts picking dandelions she'll forget about time,' the Marchesina said. 'We have an hour. There's nothing about this place that humiliates me. The vibrations are good.'

In the twilight of the shrine I drew the cool, inert air into my lungs, and with it the spices of profound antiquity. They had placed an image of St Marichiara in a deep niche; a church doll with an insipid smile peering out at us through the rust of long-dead flowers. This was the tiniest cell I had ever seen, with the walls curving in to a floor certainly less than four feet in length.

As we held each other a thought occurred to me and I gestured at our cramped surroundings. It was not possible to throw out an arm without touching the wall. 'Do you think the priestess could really have performed with a devotee in a place like this?' I asked.

'I object to the word performed,' the Marchesina said, 'but of course she could have, and did. She was infinitely pliable and so am I.'

We had an hour to ourselves and then went down the path through the pine woods to the road. I had left the car in the shade, and we sat in it and waited for the Seaweed Eater to reappear.

'I took her with us because I didn't want to spoil things,' the Marchesina said. 'She's been in a good humour ever since the funeral. It was a splendid turnout. We were in the deepest mourning with black lace, and she howled like a dog. She'll be bearable for a week at least if I'm lucky.'

'Who killed him?' I asked, suspecting that with her connections she might know something I did not know.

She turned on me clearly in surprise. 'Who killed Miraglia? Of course he killed himself.' It was a frequent affectation of hers to use the French of her supposed ancestors to emphasize a viewpoint. '*Il s'est suicidé,*' she said. 'He put on a clean shirt, made his will, washed his hands and feet and turned the family pictures to the wall.'

'In a figurative way of speaking he took his own life, in fact.'

'What does it matter by whose hand he died? This was a personal decision. He'd thrown in the sponge. His mission was over.'

This, I knew, she believed.

'And will his death make any difference?'

'Any difference to what?'

'To the way things are shaping here.'

'Apart from the funeral, which put us all in an elevated frame of mind, it would have been better if he hadn't died. My father defeated him. It would have been in all our interests to let him win.'

I looked up and saw the Seaweed Eater coming down the road, and she seemed to have undergone a change and to be hardly recognizable as the woman who had run off whimpering to leave us such a short while before, in her fear of snakes. Here as the volcano's slopes levelled off the pines drew back and the landscape opened up in soft fronded

125

glades, and youth and joy had touched the Seaweed Eater again, freeing her for an instant from the shades of the deep woods, and those of her life. She was clutching her harvest of dandelions tied up in the driving veil from which she had refused to be separated, and when she waved I saw her smile for the first time.

The Marchesina waved back. 'So everything's gone well for all of us,' she said. 'So it all turned out for the best.'

14

THE USUAL BRIEF but misleading report for transmission through channels was accompanied by the usual detailed and explanatory letter to the Colonel.

The biggest funeral for years was staged here on the 12th following the murder of the trade union leader Miraglia, who was shot several times through the heart in the town's main square at a time in the evening when it is most crowded. This was a spectacular occasion with the hearse drawn by eight splendid horses, twelve following cars and a huge expenditure on flowers by the munici-pality, most of whose members remain our original appointees, with sizeable criminal records. Led by a thirteen-man brass band playing the Dead March, the cortege traversed the principal streets, where professional mourners brought by bus from Agrigento had been placed at regular intervals. An unofficial holiday was declared and most families went off on picnics.

This is what we call here a formula killing – in other words little else but the victim's name is changed. Despite the presence of many persons in the vicinity, there were no witnesses. A suspect was arrested within hours and immediately confessed, saying that he had nothing against Miraglia, whom he did not know, and had acted under impulse. He will come up for trial in about three years, withdraw his confession, alleging that it was extracted under torture, and be discharged. Considering the implications, this might be seen as a reverse for the separatist cause, just as the crushing of the miners' strike certainly was, because it could be argued it has been proved unnecessary to appeal to the separatists to stifle such protests.

The view is growing that if there is to be an attempt to separate Sicily from Italy by force of arms the sooner this is made the better, and that there is nothing to be gained by delays.

I expected this to produce an immediate reaction, as it did, but I was flabbergasted by the form the reaction took. Two days later I picked up the phone and found myself talking to an almost flawless Italian speaker, who only betrayed the fact that he was not Italian by excessive precision in the use of the language, and a vocabulary of the kind which substitutes spouse for wife.

This was the Colonel, and I remembered the way in which he had astonished and delighted Hindu mystics by his mastery of passages from the Upanishads.

I congratulated him. 'How long have you been doing this?'

'Since our exercise was first mooted,' he said. 'Four or five months, perhaps. How do you find the accent?'

It was excellent but lifeless, and I knew he would never learn to caress the vowel in the penultimate syllable in true Italian style, not because he lacked the ear and the mimicry, but because to do so was beyond the range of his personality.

He switched to English. For a hundred or so words we had been 'thou' to each other, momentarily leaping in a Latin language the barrier of rank. Now once again we were on a less democratic footing.

'I may shortly be making an appearance in your resplendent island,' he said. 'At this stage can you hazard a guess as to when anything important is likely to happen?'

'Within a month,' I said. 'It has to.'

'In that case you'll be seeing me fairly soon,' the Colonel said.

I went to see my friend Moscato, finding him at the museum busy with his new deaf and dumb assistant packing an enormous crate, shaped like a sarcophagus. He wore a black mourning ribbon for Miraglia and this surprised me. I hadn't seen him since the murder. 'I was there,' I told him. 'Well, not quite. A hundred yards away, outside the Roma. They shot him five or six times.'

'You hear anything?' he asked.

'Nothing,' I said. 'This must have been five or ten minutes before I came on the scene.'

'Every day you become more like one of us,' Moscato said.

I took this as the compliment that was meant.

'It was something that had to be,' Moscato said. 'You will

never believe this, but in a way – try as I might – I couldn't help liking the man, and I was sorry to see him go the way he did. All the same it comes as a relief because he stirred up trouble. As far as I'm concerned he was a foreigner. He didn't understand. He thought we were corrupt, as we are, but we're all corrupt together. That way nobody loses. He was tone-deaf about our way of life.'

'He took a great liking to Sicily.'

'We had a lot to teach him. It's only a pity he couldn't have learned sooner. Enrico was here for the funeral and it's only too clear I'd lost a friend. He would only agree to stand by the coffin and hold the tassel if I left the room. I'm left with a feeling of isolation.'

I tried to cheer him up. 'The election campaign still going strong?' I asked.

'Good thing you mentioned that. It's going strong, but – get ready for it – I've changed sides.'

'You of all people? It's unbelievable. You mean you've turned the separatists in?'

'That's just what I've done. I've been backing losers all my life, and this is a lost cause if ever I saw one.'

'You've no faith in Giuliano?'

'Giuliano.' He laughed as he always did at an outrageous suggestion. 'The time's coming when they'll have had enough of him. They'll take him to a quiet place and suffocate him between two mattresses and say that he died in battle. Don't even speak about Giuliano.'

'Who are you campaigning for now, Doctor?'

'The party of corruption,' he said. 'With the Reds out of the way they're certain to win. Twenty thousand people in this town live in packing cases hammered together or in holes in the ground, and eat boiled stinging nettles and locust beans. The nuns propose to offer them a kilo of pasta

130

a head in exchange for their votes, and do you think a single one is likely to refuse? This is manna from heaven for them. Wouldn't you take it if you were in their shoes?'

'Don't tell me you're selling out for a kilo of pasta, Doctor?'

'Naturally the bribe has to be a substantial one in my case, I control twenty or thirty votes. That's worth having for any party.'

'But how do you do it? You're not a politician.'

'I help people in small ways, and they're grateful. Half the population in a dirty place like this suffer from sore places. They're usually in the most inconvenient parts of the body. I treat them with cow slobber, which costs me nothing and for which I charge nothing. It's a wonderful disinfectant. The place cleans up and the patient shakes my hand and says, "I hope to be able to do something in return one day." Well, now they can. A woman dragged herself in here a few weeks ago after she'd licked her way in fulfilment of a vow all the way from the fountain in the Square to the high altar in the church of Santa Maria. She had half a tongue left, but I saved it and she's talking again. She and her family are good for four votes. I'm the kind of person politicians like to be seen with when there's an election just round the corner.'

We had gone off leaving his assistant, with a complex sign language rigmarole, to his unpacking and now we went back to the outer office where the deaf-mute had torn the lid off the crate and was tidying away a quantity of straw in which whatever it contained had been packed. Moscato beckoned me over. 'I want to show you the first instalment of my bribe.'

Lying in what was left of the straw was what appeared at first as a waxworks dummy from some antiquated exhibition that had been broken up and auctioned off when the public had become bored with it. It was on its side and my attention was first taken by a discoloured and mildewed remnant of a scarlet cut-away coat. The eye passed instantly to what could be seen of the face, and I understood with a shock of disgust that this was no dummy. Here was a skull bursting from the tatters of resinous bandages, an eye-socket closed with a flap of shrivelled leather, a saw-edged nasal bone from which hung a single nostril, an amber tooth lodged here and there in the blackness of a mouth opened wide and wrenched sideways in a perpetual scream.

Moscato and his assistant groped delicately for a hold, turned the dummy onto its back, then as they lifted it into a standing position it hissed faintly as a dry internal detritus showered down. It could only have weighed a few pounds. Both men were full of admiration, expressed in the case of the deaf-mute by a series of winks accompanied by the ecstatic gestures of twisting the flesh of his cheek between his finger and thumb.

'They had enough of our San Severino exhibit,' Moscato said, 'but this is going to be a major attraction. They're morbid here. Anything to do with death fascinates them. They're always on the lookout for something new.'

'Where on earth did you get it from?' I asked.

'I found out that in Palermo it was the Capuchins who handed out the election largesse in support of Christian Democrat candidates. The prior heard of my following and was anxious to do business with me so he suggested I should take thirty or forty kilos of pasta and distribute them as I thought fit. I pointed out to him that my voters had already received their inducement and that I'd heard the Capuchins had a few mummies surplus to their requirements in their catacomb and would be interested to come to an arrangement. We clinched a deal on the spot.'

'Does anyone ever welsh in a case like this?' I asked. 'Can a politician who hands out an inducement be quite certain that a man will vote for him after all?'

'He can be absolutely certain,' Moscato said, 'because that is a matter of honour.'

His assistant had taken a rumpled grey topper from a bag and now stuck it at a jaunty angle on the mummy so that a half ear stuck up over the brim. I stared at this revolting cartoon of a face, asking myself whether this man's death could have been attended with the dreadful agony the face depicted or whether this was no more than the twistings and distortions produced in the cavern in which it had been dried and cured for a century and a half.

'Are you giving it a name?' I asked Moscato.

'Perhaps. If I can think of one.'

'You could label it "Born 1814. Still going strong."'

'I don't understand. What would be the point?'

'There are obscure similarities involved that might amuse some of your visitors.'

'I can't expect you to understand, but it is not amusement that we cater for.'

When I called on Crispi the widow he lived with told me, legs astraddle and hands supporting her belly, that I might find him at the post-office, adding that she had no idea when he might be back, nor did it matter to her if he failed to return. I found him crouched in the small strong-room, doing what work he could and fairly confidently awaiting a minor earth tremor which – he had been told by the government seismologist – would knock down the back of the building under which ran a 'recent tributary fault'. The post-office would then be condemned for use as a public building, although there was nothing to stop Crispi as a private citizen paying a small rent and moving into what was left of it.

Apart from this probability of improved accommodation Crispi's luck seemed on the wane, his future threatened by what was beginning to look like the separatists' loss of momentum and support. A month before, the party had scattered money and promises in all directions, but now suddenly they had been struck by caution as funds began to dry up. On the very day before Moscato and I had agreed to attend a small ceremony for the signing of the contracts of marriage with the young lady, who had undoubtedly been bullied or cajoled by her parents into becoming his wife, there was bad news. The important man who had spoken of a government post broke the news that the party's coffers were at least temporarily empty. The fortunes of war, he reminded Crispi, either for better or worse were notoriously reversible, but he would not wish to stand in Crispi's way if, etc . . .

'This,' said Crispi, 'places me in an awkward situation.' It seemed that in preliminary discussions with the girl's parents prospects-now-vanished had been examined and approved. Crispi had also been rash enough to bring up the matter of the small villa in one of the better suburbs of Catania the party organizer had suggested as an appropriate address for their legal adviser.

'A bank squeeze,' Crispi said. 'They want to put interests up and the party's not prepared to mortgage its future. My problem is what am I to tell these people?'

'The truth. What else?'

'I'm told the shortage of funds may be temporary.'

'Don't count on it. The banks don't seem so happy with the movement as they used to be.'

'As you know,' Crispi said, 'the signing's to take place at

my estate-house. I shall break the news immediately, and all I can hope is that they'll be sufficiently impressed with the property to go ahead.'

'Where is this property?' I asked. 'I've never seen it.'

'It's on what we call the lower slope.'

'Of the volcano?'

'Yes.'

'A lava field in other words?'

'Well, yes. The majority of it.'

'What does it produce?'

'Currently you could say nothing. The potential is limitless.'

'For what, Avvocato?'

'Vines. The finest vines in the country are grown on the slopes.' Crispi had a wide range of facial expressions and would have made an excellent salesman had salesmanship not been disapproved of among the professional classes. 'Production is low, but quality extremely high. The wines are light, graceful and aromatic. There's never enough to go round.'

'How many vines have you planted so far?'

'None,' he said. 'We'll be making a start in the next two or three years. The volcanic soil as you know takes three centuries to season. It's just about ready.'

'And having planted your vines how long before you begin to harvest the grapes?'

'Say five years. There should be some small return by then.'

He thought about it. 'Well, largely as I've lived in the past, I imagine.'

'But now you'll have a wife to support. She'll expect you to buy her smart dresses.'

'I'll find some way of doing that. Mind you, she's not the

kind to ask for a great deal.'

'Tell me about your prospective in-laws. They're poor people, I imagine.'

'Yes, but they're the possessors of a natural dignity that transcends class barriers. Peasant origin, if you will, but it's something that's not immediately apparent. They have great taste and discrimination.'

'And the girl's a bit of a beauty, I suppose?'

'Yes, probably you'd say she was. But that's the least of it. For me the real attraction's her fine character. She's down to earth. She has a sense of humour, which is something I enormously admire. Our life will be based upon mutual respect, and that being so I don't see that it can go wrong. Whatever they may say about the age difference it has the makings of a success.'

15

'THIS IS MY LAST line of defence,' Crispi said.

The three of us, Moscato included, stood at the foot of a great, black slope, receding in an ever narrowing sash to the cone of the volcano, seventeen miles away. There was no landscape the volcano could not counterfeit in a small, sectional way, be it a sliver of crystalline desert or an alpine glade with mosses trailing from the branches of the trees. But this was what one remembered it by: a torrent of lava that had flowed from the crater and burned everything in black, glistening clinkers. Its surface had changed hands many times, despite the three centuries required to convert the lava into the richest and most fruitful of land, for the possession of a sizeable lava bed enabled its owner to describe himself as *possedente*, and as a member of the land-owning class to claim tax advantages and privileges, including in Palma the right to cross the Piazza Vittoria on horseback, and in the past immunity from capital punishment for crimes, excluding witchcraft and sodomy.

Two or three hundred yards to the left of Crispi's barren acres, beautiful trees artfully contorted in Japanese fashion grew on a patch of good red earth. Here, there was nothing but blackness. Sunlight rippled like a shallow stream over the rocks. Crispi repeated, 'This is my last line of defence.'

'I can hardly believe what you're telling us,' Moscato said. 'How old did you say this girl is?'

'Fifteen,' Crispi said. 'But she's very advanced for her age. Her parents agree that it's a good thing for her.'

'I simply don't understand why you have to get married,' Moscato said. 'Explain to me again what all this is about.'

'As you know, my main source of income has come to an end,' Crispi said. 'The post-war rush for ancestors is over. The job the party found for me has fallen through. I call this my estate, but it isn't really. It was left to me in my aunt's will on condition I married and produced an heir within five years.'

'It's a pitiful story,' Moscato said, 'and I don't believe a word of it. You've just made it up. All you want is an excuse to screw a young girl. I feel faint in this heat. For heaven's sake let's find some shade.'

'We can sit in the house,' Crispi said.

The house was a squat, stone building with a few scales of grey paint stuck here and there to the cracked wooden surfaces of the boarded-up window and the door.

'I made arrangements for this to be tidied up,' Crispi said, 'but nobody seems to have done anything about it.' He wrenched open the door to release the ancient staleness of a cavern, and a huge spider crept into sight round the jamb, dazzled possibly by the sunshine, before scuttling back. Crispi peered into the gloom. 'The furniture seems to have been spirited away,' he said.

'Let's take a walk,' Moscato said. 'Perhaps we can make it to the trees over there before getting sunstroke.'

We started to clamber over the lava. 'Once the house is fixed up it should be very pleasant,' Crispi said. 'The view in the other direction is entrancing, and the air up here is exceptionally pure.'

'Has this poor girl any idea of what she's in for?' Moscato said. 'This sounds to me like an arranged marriage of the most deplorable kind. Have you actually met?'

'On a number of occasions,' Crispi said. 'I'm not altogether antediluvian when it comes to things like this. Nobody would describe this as a tempestuous courtship; on the other hand we respect each other and we're realists. These are decent people living in somewhat depressed circumstances. The parents may be relieved in a way to get their daughter off their hands. She's called Isabella.'

'That's a pretty name,' I said. 'Uncommon.'

'It suits her,' Crispi said. 'She's an unusual girl. Upright in all her dealings, and pure in spirit.'

'My heart bleeds for her. What's wrong with the widow? Couldn't you have married her?' Moscato asked.

Crispi's rounded but flabby cheeks shook like a jelly as he ruled out the possibility. 'It's bad enough as it is. There's never less than three kids in the bed with us. I can't stomach the idea of it. This gives me a chance to get out of her clutches.'

We crunched and stumbled uphill over the lava. It was hard to believe that there could be a hotter, drier place on earth than this. Extraordinary weeds had colonized the area, protecting themselves with an armament of devices against assaults of any kind. I had never set eyes on most of them before. In spite of his boredom and irritation Moscato's interest was awakened by plants known to him, that exuded toxic saps when damaged, were covered in stinging hairs, had armed themselves with poisonous spines capable of lethally injecting a small mammal. Others – from our point of view the most objectionable – shot volleys of hooked burrs in all directions when disturbed. The place sizzled with cicadas – a sound which seemed to emphasize the great shadeless heat. Something whisked out of sight, dislodging a few small clinkers among the lava. 'You see a snake once in a while,' Crispi said. 'Always remember they're more nervous of you than you are of them.'

'What's the purpose of these poor, deluded persons' visit?' Moscato asked.

'To look over the property, and discuss the marriage contract. They'll bring a lawyer and there may be papers to sign, in which case you can act as witnesses.'

'But I don't quite see what you get out of this. Suppose you manage in the end to produce an heir? An heir to what? This isn't an inheritance, it's a desert.'

'Our eyes are fixed on posterity. In fifty years' time this will be a vineyard. As far as the eye can see.'

We had reached the shade of the twisted birches, and spent a few minutes picking the hooked balls the weeds had thrown at us off each other's clothing, before slumping down. The great spread of lava had narrowed to a bottleneck here. At this hour of the day the cone of the volcano bore a dull metallic sheen, as if hammered from zinc. Here and there in the distance houses stood in islands that had been miraculously bypassed by the tides of lava. They were by custom defiantly overpainted and their eaves and balconies carved with redoubtable animals – bears, wild-boars and lions – and the pagan symbols of the conquering sun which the Church forebade. I could hear the yelping and snapping of the brave, ugly dogs kept chained up, as they snuffled and pawed as if for truffles after the warning vibrations buried deep in the earth.

From the nearest house came in addition a garbled operatic aria bellowed through a window into the sea of clinkers. The sound was harsh and leathery, and there was a screeching urgency about it, reminding one of the performance of a bagpipe player about to run out of breath. The singing was followed by peals of laughter. Moscato seemed startled and Crispi smiled a tepid reassurance.

'My neighbour,' he explained.

'Why does he sing like that?' Moscato asked.

'To defeat fear,' Crispi told him.

Moscato shook his head, wincing. 'He's mad,' he said.

'He lives a very isolated life.'

'Let's try to be frank with one another, as well as ourselves,' Moscato said. 'Let's suppose that, incredibly enough, this land ever becomes yours. Could you find a buyer for it?'

'Certainly,' Crispi said. 'It would be wiser to hold on to it for a few years to benefit from its full potential.'

'You'd be insane to do so. Take the first offer anybody is deluded enough to make, and go on your way rejoicing.'

'I'm grateful as ever for your advice,' Crispi said sourly. 'When the time comes we'll discuss the matter again.'

By the time we got back to Crispi's shack the family had arrived – an hour before the appointed time. They amazed me. After three or four generations of hoeing the land all day and sleeping in a grotto, cramped up like corpses in a

Bronze-Age mound burial, Sicilians begin to change their shape. They get shorter and thicker, developing broad, powerful shoulders and short legs. Their faces widen across the cheekbones and their eyes narrow in the flatness of the surrounding flesh like those of Peruvian Indians or Eskimos. An increasingly swarthy complexion is further darkened and tinged with something resembling a high-altitude purplish flush. Both the man and his wife conformed to this stunted American-Indian appearance, but the girl was a complete throw-back; different in every way, a head and shoulders taller than her parents – a giantess by local standards who had refused to adapt. At the introductions she bobbed us something like a curtsy, then thrust out a huge red hand to each in turn, in which Crispi's small paw was entirely enveloped. She had freed herself from whatever it was, visible in her parents' expressions, that kept them permanently on guard. She cupped the wide mouth to conceal a giggle, fidgetted a little, twisted and turned, dabbed at a spot at the corner of a nostril, then slouched off with her mother to inspect what Crispi had described as his estate-house. Crispi had drawn aside for a discussion with the family's lawyer, a gangling and seemingly embarrassed young man who was taken by a paroxysm of coughing after listening to what Crispi had to tell him. 'What am I going to do with him?' Moscato whispered. 'Even a dozen injections can't produce a miracle. She's twice his size. Imagine our old friend with all his willingness and determination getting into bed with her. She'll crush the life out of him. Something has to be done. If only I could find him some job with the party of corruption to tide him over. I'll ring the Prior and see if he has any suggestion to make.'

The father came out of the house dragging a splintered table with cobwebs hanging like small fishing nets from its legs. He pointed back into the darkness. 'Bats in there,' he said.

Crispi put on a squeamish expression. 'We'll get rid of them. Chase them away.'

'Watch out they don't find a way back,' the man said. 'They poison the air.'

He put a newspaper-wrapped bundle on the table, untied it to remove a loaf of flat, peasant bread, and then began to unroll a long grey cloth in which a second object was swaddled, to disclose ricotta cheese. He took a red handkerchief as large as a flag from his pocket and wiped the dust from the surface of the table. Next he drew a knife, began to cut the bread into chunks, and gestured to us smilingly to help ourselves. There was a bottle of wine, too, properly corked, and a knife appeared in his hand and the cork flew into the air. Moscato, mentioning his heartburn, held himself aloof, but the rest of us helped ourselves to the bread and ricotta – Crispi, hungry as at all times, with avidity. The father ate like a crocodile, the hard, crusted bread instantly crushed and pulverized in his neanderthal jaws. There was a US Army tin mug for those who preferred not to drink out of a bottle. The wine had been made in peasant style, with a twig of the vine with a few leaves attached to increase its body and improve its thirst-quenching properties, and only two mouthfuls were required to fur the inside of the teeth.

The father watched each of us in turn, summed us up and placed us in our categories in the archives of his mind. I suspected him of possessing that special kind of intelligence that is destroyed or at least weakened by education, something not wholly separated from animal instinct – the inbred resource of a nomadic Australoid who discovers water in the hearts of plants and will never starve while there are

143

sustaining roots under the earth. He called everybody 'your honour' without a trace of servility. 'So this is your estate, your honour?' he said to Crispi, thereafter wandering away with a stick to poke about among the lava and pick up and sniff something he had found. By this time the lawyer had passed on the bad news.

He came back. 'The vines require a clear fifty centimetres for their roots. If you had a few sons, your honour, you could basket up earth and get them started. In our case God sent nothing but girls.'

'Who are you voting for?' Moscato asked him. 'The party of corruption?'

The man nodded, adding an out-of-date civility, 'With your permission.'

'What's the going rate at the moment?' Moscato said.

'Money doesn't enter into it in our case,' the man said. 'The landlord's offered to change our living quarters.'

'You've done better than me. I only got a spare mummy from the catacombs out of it so far. I understand you're in a grotto? Are you on the lookout for something more spacious?'

'Our daughter couldn't sleep in the niche where we were. She was getting curvature of the spine, and they won't let you enlarge it. Now they're moving us out things are looking up.'

'Why's she so big?' Moscato asked.

'We overfed her when she was young, your honour. We lost the three other girls, so after that we gave her their share of the food as well as her own.'

'Well, that's a reasonable precaution,' Moscato said, 'and it seems to have been a success.'

While we had been engaged with the father, the girl had dashed off, dragging her mother after her, on a quick tour of

144

inspection of the place. She had pushed open the door of the house and for the third time the enormous spider shot into sight, then drew itself back. Using a sharp fragment of lava she had stopped to scratch her initials on a cactus, then she and her mother had gone on to encircle Crispi and the Avvocato Lupo, studying Crispi from all angles, longing, I suspected, to be able to feel his muscles and to learn the worst of what awaited her under the jacket, well-laundered but patched on one elbow, and the cotton trousers that hardly disguised the spindly outlines of Crispi's legs, and were buttoned so tightly over the sagging and empty inflation of the belly.

'Giving him the once-over,' Moscato said. 'I should have thought one look would have been enough. Lively youngster, isn't she? I've taken quite a fancy to her myself.'

Isabella danced behind Crispi's back, making faces in her father's direction, her mother trying to pull her away. 'Nothing she'd like better than to give him the lame mule treatment,' Moscato whispered in my ear. He cuffed at a horse-fly. They had smelt out our presence; one landed on Crispi's arm and the girl flattened it instantly with the practised skill of one who has lived among them. Crispi smiled up at her weakly. He seemed unusually pale.

Moscato captured the father. 'How's it going?'

'We're talking about one thing and another,' the man said.

'But no conclusion?'

'These things take time.'

'Has anybody asked your daughter whether she wants to live in a place like this?'

'Not so far, sir.'

'Would *you*?'

'I'd do what I was told if I was a girl. That's the way it's always been.'

'The young aren't like that now. They say what they think.'

'It's quiet up here, sir. I'll admit that.'

'Avvocato Crispi has a chance to take over the post-office, but it suffers from subsidences.'

'You mean it isn't safe?'

'That's what I mean.'

'Could I make a suggestion? We have a lot of good neighbours down in the grottoes. Maybe if we sign up as arranged the Avvocato would consider coming to live down there. Whatever people tell you about the grottoes, they're not too bad. You can get the light put in if you want to spend a little money, and there's running water from a spigot a couple of hundred yards away.'

The man went off, supposedly to discuss the new possibilities with his wife. 'Did you hear that?' I said to Moscato. 'What an extraordinary suggestion.'

Moscato seemed surprised that I should be surprised. 'Haven't you any idea of what's going on?' he asked.

'I obviously haven't.'

'Wait a moment, and you'll see. They're supposed to be arriving at a basis for agreement, but you can forget about that. It's all over. All that's left now is a face-saving exercise. I don't want to have to listen to provisos and caveats and lex non-scriptas, and I can't stand this heat any longer. I'm going over there to tell them to make their minds up. With a little luck we may find out that things aren't so bad as they seemed.'

He went over and joined Crispi and Avvocato Lupo, joined in the hand-waving and shoulder-shrugging and came back looking as though a load had been lifted from his shoulders. Lupo stuffed some papers into his wallet, and he and Crispi began to follow slowly.

'What's happened?' I asked.

'They want a month or so to think things over, which means it's all off.'

'What a blow for poor old Crispi.'

'Not a bit of it,' Moscato said. 'It's a relief. He had a narrow shave and he knows it. Didn't you notice? He was shaking like a leaf. You'd have thought she was going to eat him.'

'If he didn't like her why didn't he pull out? Why let it go as far as this?'

'He told us he'd seen her before, but he hadn't. This was the first meeting and he was scared stiff of her. I thought he was going to faint when she swatted that horsefly.'

'What put the prospective in-laws off?' I asked.

'Everything,' Moscato said. 'If he had anything to offer they would have taken him on, but he had nothing. They could see their daughter wasn't even going to get two square meals out of it. Didn't you see the old man checking on the clinkers? If the girl stands a chance of being buried under the post-office she's better off to stay where she is in the grottoes.'

'Why go through the charade of suggesting Crispi might go and live down in the grottoes with them?'

'Because they're civilized people with a tradition of good manners. Can you imagine a man like that saying to us we can't allow our daughter to marry your friend because he's old, he's ugly, and he's poor? Instead, they put the onus on him. They know they're quite safe, and nobody's feelings are hurt.'

Crispi and the lawyer had been joined by the family and an exchange of expansive gestures followed by vigorous hand-shaking made it clear that everything had been settled in an amicable fashion.

'Let's go home and try to put all this out of our minds,' Moscato said.

16

SUDDENLY I FELT EMERGE an inexplicable something in my relationship with the Marchesina, hinting at a mysterious contact between our minds for which I understood that no concrete evidence could ever be found. Repeatedly I had the sensation that she was eavesdropping on my thoughts, and it was one that filled me with speculative unease. When on the verge of broaching some new topic I would find her forestalling me, even breaking into my inner dialogue to offer solutions to questions I had not posed. The Colonel, I knew, would have been in his element in such a situation, eager with controlled experiments and pseudo-scientific explanations. I was less happy.

'So you'll be leaving us quite soon,' she said.

'Will I?' I said. 'I don't recall saying anything about it.'

'Whatever you're doing here is coming to an end and you've been trying to make up your mind what to do next.'

'And have I decided yet?'

'No,' she said. 'You will soon. You're a person who can't settle to anything for long. Sicily hasn't quite matched up to your expectations the second time round. I expect you'll go.'

It was probably to be explained by her sensitivity and her powers of observation. No chance remark of mine, no change of mood could elude her assessment. Yet it was strange that only that very morning I had reached the conclusion that the time had come to be quite frank with the Colonel, no longer concealing my opinion that the end of our mission was in sight.

'As I've already told you, I never gave it more than a year.'

'It will be much less,' she said.

'Have you by any chance been looking up my horoscope?' I asked. Horoscopes enthralled her. It was all she bothered to read in the newspapers, and she was by no means discouraged when I described how so many of them were mass-produced in my friend Placido's small factory with its beautiful view of Montelepre and the stars.

'I've been studying both our horoscopes,' she said, 'and that's what they say.'

She had suddenly produced the splendid news that out of the blue the Seaweed Eater, perpetual encumbrance in our relationship, had begun to blow up with another false pregnancy, and was about to be rushed off to hospital in Catania for this to be dealt with. Freedom beckoned, but unhappily her indisposition coincided with the Marchesina's turn for the use and enjoyment of the furniture held in common by the four palaces, but the ancient retainers still employed in them lacked the strength to shift heavy objects.

'We can't stay here,' she said. 'In any case I have to get away. I need fresh scenes, action, stimulation. For me this place is no better than an open prison, and when you go it will become a closed one. Let's go on a long journey.'

I knew that any adventure she proposed was likely to be strenuous. Since the episode at the shrine of Venus she had lured me away on a brief but exhausting tunny-fishing trip, in which – the Seaweed Eater included – we had bloodied ourselves in an all-night carnage with three hours for sleep snatched on the nets piled up on deck, full of gore and fleas.

'No more shrines,' I said. 'No more massacres of fish.'

'I have to live while I can. Let's go to Lipari.'

'Why Lipari?'

'It's full of released criminals who are not allowed to return to the mainland.'

'Well?' I asked.

'All these men are innocent. They inherited the vendetta like an heirloom and they carried out their obligations knowing that they would be repaid by society by being locked away in a cell for half their lives. They are saints. Once my father took me to visit one of these men who was a relative. He carried out his obligation when he was twenty years old, and by that time he was fifty, and it was thirty years since he had looked into the blue of the sky. "I am neither alive nor dead," he said. "I stand in the presence of God. He never speaks to me, but sometimes he smiles."'

'Why should I go to Lipari?' I asked. 'I don't want to be depressed.' Suddenly I remembered the Seaweed Eater and my salvation. 'The Seaweed Eater will be out of hospital in two days. She'll expect you to be there waiting for her when she gets back. In any case Lipari's too far away. We'd be travelling non-stop, there and back.'

'We'll make it San Stefano, then.'

151

I was immediately suspicious. 'And what does San Stefano have to offer by way of stimulation?'

'It's a Franciscan monastery. The brothers were in the news just before you came back. They occasionally accept guests and it would be interesting to spend the night there. It's really no distance at all. Why not pick me up at six?'

I had to agree, but made a quick call at the post-office to check with Crispi what this expedition was likely to involve. 'All monks are scoundrels,' he said. 'These made a bit more of a splash than most.' It was a typical anti-clerical outburst which I dismissed. He told me what he could remember of the details of their villainies. 'It could be a strange experience,' he said, 'and I'd like to be coming with you.'

He was remarkably cheerful about his recent reverse. 'My pride's a little dented,' he said. 'What can you expect? Still, I'll soon get over it. I'm one of those people who bounce back. Perhaps it was a blessing in disguise. There's a young person employed here who's expressed an interest in my work – so who knows?'

It was a stiff drive to San Stefano through bare mountains, as aloof in their black aridity as the tips and slagheaps of an ugly industrialism. The monastery came into sight, a battlemented pile on a hilltop over a sudden breakthrough of green fields; sited here for defence against a succession of marauders on their way to more rewarding targets. There were monks everywhere hard at work, strapping bearded men ploughing with oxen, planting and weeding, scything grass, hewing wood, forking up steaming manure. The intensely physical and athletic aspect of their activity corrected a mental image of devotional calm. A gigantic Franciscan with a 12-bore tucked under his arm stood watching this scene, like a guard in charge of a chain-gang.

It was a sight that clearly filled the Marchesina with admiration and surprise.

A young brother awaited us at the gate. By comparison with the strident masculinity of the monks at work in the fields, his manner was meek and shifty. He listened distantly to what the Marchesina had to say, his large teeth gleaming through the tangled down of his beard.

'We have no suitable arrangements for visitors,' he said.

'I wish to see the Abbot,' the Marchesina told him.

Several demented-looking cows charged past chased by a monk screeching like an Arab herdsman and thwacking at their haunches with his stick. 'The price would be four hundred lire per person,' the young brother said.

'Twice the rate for a hotel in Palermo,' the Marchesina protested.

'Yes, but here there is nowhere else to go.'

His face was quite unlined, and as smooth as wax, and his eyes were soft and vacant like those of a gentle animal such as a gazelle, liable to take sudden fright. A sharp tang of ammonia, exhaled by the mountains of dung at our backs, lay heavy on the air. The young brother's top lip lifted slightly as if in a weak, unpractised approach to a smile. 'These are our rules,' he said.

Silence, he announced, with huge respect for the word, was the rule imposed here, except in the refectory, where ten minutes were allocated to the evening meal taken at five. Thereafter the monks occupied themselves with their devotions until retiring for the night at seven, but there was nothing for the visitor to do except, having removed his shoes, to pace stealthily to and fro in the ambulatory. He warned us that we would be locked in our cells for the night, although a bell was provided to summon the brother on night-duty in case of emergency. Part of the rule was that we should rid the monastery of our presence before matins on the following day.

We walked barefoot as instructed, in an anti-clockwise direction in proper meditative fashion in the cloister, repeatedly overtaken by some burly brother shuffling past at high speed. No words passed between the monks but one would grunt loudly as he overtook and passed another, and there were flamboyant exchanges of gestures that might have been taken as ribald or even obscene. No notice was taken of us.

After we had completed some dozen circuits the young brother from the gate reappeared to take us to the refectory where he seated us at a long table upon which platters of bread, ricotta and onions flanked by jugs of water had been set out, before hurrying away. Within moments a bell rang, the door burst open and the monks stormed in to take possession of the far end of the table, and all the noise that had been banished from these surroundings was back. The monks pounced on the food, elbowed each other, scuffled and shoved. Spoons rattled, there were juvenile whoopings, cries of real or mock anger, protests. Brothers, having emptied the nearest platters, were scampering up and down the table to raid those beyond their reach. They wrestled for possession of bread and used their sandals to ward off piratical attacks. The room had filled with the odours of staling hay, cow-byres and sweat.

The Marchesina was entertained. 'The life they lead,' she explained. 'Hard work, plain food and close contact with the earth.'

'This doesn't surprise you in any way?'

'It's no more than I expected,' she said.

An ancient ecclesiastic had fumbled his way into the room, clearly indifferent to the uproar. He tottered to a chair at the head of the table, dropped into it, and appeared to fall asleep. 'The Abbot,' the Marchesina said. 'His predecessor was beheaded on this very table.'

I was prepared and waiting for this. 'It couldn't have been the same one. You're speaking of something that happened twenty years ago. This table's new.'

'So you know all about it?'

'I thought I ought to make a few enquiries. Crispi told me about last year's trial, from which I gather things are much as ever.'

'They were acquitted,' she said, 'to the joy and relief of all San Stefano.'

'On charges of extortion and kidnapping, wasn't it?'

'There was a charge of murder, too, which the prosecution decided to drop.'

The bell rang again. All the monks got up together, some still clutching hunks of bread, and began to rush for the door, and we heard them stampede away down the passage into the echoings and then the silence of the building's great vaulted chambers. After a moment the old Abbot roused himself. He picked up an unpeeled onion, bit into it, then got up shakily to follow them. The door closed softly behind them. The Marchesina laughed, seemingly satisfied by the performance. Distantly a sweet and solemn chanting had begun.

We were released from our cells at four-thirty and set out on the return journey at dawn, by which time the monks, brandishing sticks and uttering furious cries, were already driving their cows out into the pastures.

'The trial, according to Crispi,' I said, 'was concluded in an atmosphere of persistent hysteria. Extra police had to be brought in to prevent any attempt by the peasant crowds to set the defendants free. A photograph taken clandestinely in court and reproduced in a newspaper purported to show haloes round several of the accused men's heads. Naturally this doesn't astonish you in any way.'

'No,' she said, 'not in the slightest.'

'Did they kidnap people?'

'My guess is they did.'

'And carry out acts of extortion against rich landlords?'

'The two things go together.'

'And, as charged, they kept prostitutes in their cells?'

'They are men.'

'Why do you suppose the peasants were so solidly on their side?'

'They don't steal from peasants because peasants have nothing to steal, and nothing makes them so happy as to see someone taking it out of the rich. They worship them for their strength. Let me explain that good and evil don't count for anything in places like San Stefano. Or put it this way, if you're strong you're good. The strong make their own laws, and the weak respect them.'

'Yes,' I said. 'That about sums up the island philosophy. Would it be an exaggeration to say that you yourself have a certain respect for the brothers?'

'I feel an instinctive reaction to their power,' she said. 'But this is something you can't understand. It's a very Sicilian thing.'

And the fact was that try as I might I did not understand it. I did battle with it. I came to terms with it, but I could see at this moment, and following this experience, that this was an incessant drama without intermissions in which I would always lack the understanding to play any role other than that of onlooker.

We drove on through nature's ugly counterfeit of a wasteland of man's making and I thought about the past and of the future. The Marchesina's strangely renewed zest was ill-matched with my own interlude of weariness. It was a moment of our association when I recalled the time when, at the war's end, I had been offered a remarkable house on a cliff's edge near Ragusa. 'Buy it,' the locals said. 'It's going for nothing.'

I took a friend along to ask his advice. The view everyone raved about was of a rock pinnacle known as U Vicchione (the Old Man) rising a thousand feet sheer from the sea. I handed my friend a pair of 12-power binoculars at the precise moment when one of Europe's last sea eagles perched on its summit drew the wedge of its tail-feathers tight and unfolded its enormous wings, about to take off.

He passed the glasses back, and shook his head. 'Overpowering,' he said. 'It's far too beautiful.'

'Is that possible?'

'You want to settle permanently in a place like this?'

'That was my intention.'

'After three months this view would overpower you. You'd sit with your back to it, and then you'd move into a room facing the other direction. To live in a house you don't need eagles. You need swallows under the eaves. Forget about it. This isn't for you. What's wrong with a moment of calm in one's life?'

17

MOSCATO SENT LO BIANCO, a deserter from the separatist army in the east, to see me. The doctor had given him a note. 'I know you're still interested in this stupid business,' the note said, 'so what this man has to say may be of use to you. It will give you some idea of the quality of the leadership of the movement I managed to rescue myself from.'

'They're out of cash,' Lo Bianco said. 'No more and no less than that. You can't fight a war with promises and threats. Their mistake was to tell the banks what was in store for them, and that was the end of the handouts. What could they expect?'

He had been in tanks in the disastrous campaign in Cyrenaica, branded by the African sun which had left crows-feet like dried-up watercourses, and pale eyelids in the thin dark mask of his face. In the Italian army he had been a senior sergeant. Concetto Gallo, leader of the separatist forces in the east, had put him in command of the armour with rank of major. This was the first inside account of the activities and intentions of the second front of the separatist forces, and as I listened to what he had to say I abandoned hope for them. 'I asked to inspect the armoured vehicles,' Lo Bianco said, 'and was taken to a cowshed where they had hidden a single tank under bales of hay. Nobody could start it, and I found that rats had gnawed the insulation off the electrical wiring.' He looked as tired as though he'd come out of a long battle, but what had worn him out had been standing around and worrying about the future. Gallo had taken him on a tour of the camp where he saw a lot of men in brand-new American uniforms mooching about with their hands in their pockets, spitting on the ground. Gallo said they were recruits that had just come in. In addition to their uniforms these men wore the most beautiful new American boots, and they had been supplied, as part of the military package-deal, with enough dried milk to last at least five years. There should have been a delivery of arms at the same time, Gallo explained, but they had gone astray and were believed to have been sold off to agents working for the rebels in Greece. Lo Bianco showed surprise that nobody saluted them, and Gallo said, 'We let them off that. They're all officer-cadets from good families, and they regard saluting as servile.' Lo Bianco had then asked to be taken to see the ordinary soldiers.

He found them in a camp situated on an abandoned estate consisting largely of the De Mauro mountain, which was covered with tangled thickets. This second category of

159

troops wore no uniforms at all and were billeted in a ram-shackle estate-house with no glass in the windows, snakes all over the place, and the drinking water spoiled because a sheep had fallen into the well. Men were lying on the floor trying to sleep. The doors were barricaded so they had to climb in through the windows. None of them had shaved for days. To save themselves the trouble of climbing in and out of the place in the night they pissed in a corner, and the smell was terrible. One man had a couple of lambs with him he refused to be parted from. '"What are all these supposed to be?" I asked. "Ex-bandits," Gallo said frankly. "In course of regeneration."

'A day or two later,' Lo Bianco continued, 'Gallo came to see me and told me, "A problem has arisen over food. We've run out of everything. Our backers have let us down. What do we do in a situation like this?"

'"We adopt the correct military procedure," I said. "We print requisitioning-orders, and commandeer supplies in the proper legal fashion. The orders are retained by their recipients and serve as receipts, and compensation is paid in due course."

'Gallo used to say, "Always remember that first and foremost I'm a professor of history." He told me he'd written a book about Napoleon's campaign in Italy, but was only interested in military theory and never bothered to go into details such as requisitioning. "Where do the supplies come from?" he wanted to know. I told him they came from wherever they were to be found, and that contributions would have to be levied on the local farmers. He asked me if we were likely to meet with resistance, and I told him, yes, probably. Farmers objected to having their cows and sheep driven away. What could I say? The next thing was who would do the requisitioning? Would we send the gentlemen-

160

volunteers who would make a better impression? I told him it wasn't the impression but the results that mattered, and that as we were down to the last of our salted horseflesh it might be better to settle for the bandits; besides which, none of the gentlemen volunteers, being townsmen, could ride. Gallo agreed with this, and said he'd go with them because it would be a chance to try out a race-horse that someone had knocked off. He put on a city suit so as not to draw attention to himself, he said, and at that point I was sure he was really out of his mind. One of the bandits who'd been in the army took a flame-thrower along to demonstrate how to use it. When a landowner refused to hand over anything they poured petrol over the floor of his wine store, the bandit aimed the flame-thrower through the window, and the building blew up and killed him.'

'By which time,' I said, 'you'd had enough?'

'I'd had all I could take. They'd posted sentries all round the camp with orders to shoot deserters. It wasn't easy to get away.'

'Do you think Giuliano can save the situation?' I asked.

A link-up between the two forces was now seen in the press as the separatists' last hope if they went for a military solution. There were two obstacles to this. The first was the many mountain ranges separating them and the second the striking divergence in their aims. From being a bandit Giuliano now saw himself as a reformer dedicated in however muddled a fashion to the cause of the poor. Gallo and his backers were reactionaries and romantics pledged to the rediscovery of a feudalistic or even pre-feudalistic world inhabited by fair ladies and Arthurian knights, but nothing else of importance by way of a population.

'They've given him up and he's given them up,' Lo Bianco said.

'Giuliano came down to San Mauro while I was there. They'd heard about his craze for hygiene so they spent a week scrubbing the place up and getting rid of thousands of turds. All the bandits had to wash and shave themselves and Gallo made the volunteers learn to present arms. Giuliano turned up in his white mackintosh and they were all lined up ready for inspection, but he didn't even look at them. All he wanted to do was to see over the camp, and there was no way of distracting his attention from anything he wasn't supposed to notice. He found the old tank in the cowshed, but made no comment, and he was just passing a store where they kept the wood when he asked for it to be opened up, and there was a girl inside. She'd been picked up at one of the farms on the requisitioning trip and kept locked up there ever since. He asked what she was doing there. Gallo tried to make a joke of it and said, "She came with the rations." "Did she ask to come?" Giuliano had wanted to know, and she'd yelled out, "No, I didn't. Those animals kidnapped me, and I'm abused all the time." Gallo was looking pretty sick by this time. Giuliano asked him if he knew that this had been going on, and Gallo said he hadn't known until this moment that the girl was being held against her will, and would see to it that she was sent home immediately.

'Giuliano said to him in front of everybody, "In Montelepre we shoot people who do this sort of thing." That was more or less the end of the visit, and you could see that Giuliano had lost interest, even if he'd ever had it.'

Four days later there was a message from the Colonel, whom I knew could not be held off indefinitely, calling me to Palermo. 'Do you think I should be there?' he had asked, and although I did not, I knew that sooner or later he would come – and here he was. We had an office in the island capital looked after by a pretty girl in uniform who had once driven a general from battlefield to battlefield and had volunteered to stay on to wind down a romance with a local boy. There was some mix-up with dates, she told me, and the Colonel was up at Monreale where the Normans had built the most splendid of their churches on the top of a small mountain five miles out of town.

I drove up there and parked the car in an anguished street carved into the face of a near-precipice just off the Piazza della Cattedrale, from which there was a bird's-eye view over the Conca d'Oro, which is the greatest and most glorious orchard and market garden in the world. Although there was nothing of gold about it except the roofs of houses on nearby slopes, it frothed, bubbled and exploded with the voluptuous greenery of millions of trees and plants. No African winds can reach here to pelt the fields and streets with locusts. Mists are drawn up everywhere from the swampiness towards the sun, the sweat refuses to dry on the skin and one treads sticky white blossoms underfoot. This is another world from Palma. Faces and characters have been formed and softened in the damp air. No comedy enters into local lives, nor are they basically ferocious in the way of the people of the east shore who came from the sea. Down in Palma innumerable generations have learned to live with a volcano; a precarious relationship that has buttressed and braced their characters. In Monreale they play calm, reflective games and scopa is barred. There are no witches. Nobody wears coral except for purposes of innocent decoration. They eat from necessity or gluttony, never to gain magical strength from their food, and they can be comfortable in the knowledge that it contains no sinister additives by persons motivated by lust or hate. Love-making itself is less cerebral and calculated, and whereas in Palma those

163

who may have had enough of love as well as life customarily throw themselves in a gesture of utter finality from a cliff, in Monreale they favour an overdose, which frequently proves ineffective.

Monreale is one of those small, concentrated towns where everybody passes through the main square several times a day, and I settled myself outside the small triangular café on the hilltop in the expectation of seeing the Colonel there sooner or later.

It was early evening, time by local custom to sip the calming, cooling drinks blended from the juices of a variety of fruits. What appeared at first glance to be beautiful women paraded singly at this hour. From the warnings I had received I took them to be transvestites – also a production, it was said, of the special climate – but there was no way of knowing this for certain as their dresses were designed to conceal evidences of muscle. Beggars passed in endless procession, some of them fearfully mutilated by the wars or the mines, squirming along on legless trunks, leather pads strapped to their buttocks, or trundled by assistants, spread-eagled on castor-mounted boards. After a while I wanted to free myself from these sights, so I went on a quick tour of the streets in the hope of running the Colonel to earth, and then gave up and went into the Cathedral.

Repairs were going on to the main structure of the building and the entrance door was closed by a wooden barrier. There was a great deal of activity inside, making it likely that I should pass unnoticed, so I squeezed round the barrier and went into the aisle and then into the nave. Here scaffolding covered part of the walls, and serious-faced men who were clearly specialists were at work cleaning mosaic tableaux of scenes from the Old Testament. I stood watching them at work for a moment, then suddenly I spotted the Colonel up there with the experts on the scaffolding, refurbishing a panel depicting the episode of Noah's drunkenness. I called to him, 'John,' and he looked down and saw me and waved his sketch-pad. 'Be with you in a jiffy,' he called back.

In a moment he dropped his sketching pad into a satchel and climbed down the ladder. He gave me a firm handshake and a benevolent smile, and once again it struck me how much his face resembled an ikon, its features drawn with the extreme regularity of ancient art, the three identical lines incised under each of the mild blue eyes, the stiff but copious grey hair parted in the centre, and combed back behind the ears in the scrupulous locks of the twelfth century.

'John,' he said, 'it was so nice of you to come. Was it today? So sorry you should have had to drag yourself all the way up here. One of the prebendaries slipped me in when backs were turned. A huge piece of luck. How are you after your various experiences? Do forgive me for being a nuisance. Lovely to see you.'

The innocent eyes radiated enthusiasm. 'People can be so charming,' he said. 'The prebendary pitched an extraordinary story about my being a visiting expert from the British Museum. I shouldn't be at all surprised if nobody believed a word of it, but they were all so frightfully civilized. Perhaps I should dump these things and we can go somewhere and have a chat.'

He led the way under an arch cut in a forest of glittering animals into a white-washed room used by the workmen, put down his satchel and went into the lavatory to wash his hands. The satchel was open, and I slipped out the pad for a quick glance at his sketches and was filled with admiration for their professional quality. A moment later he was back. 'Let's go and find a coffee,' he said.

'I don't want to drag you away,' I told him. 'Why don't I come back?'

'Nice of you, but I was going to call it a day. The light's getting bad. I'm sure these kind people will let me come back tomorrow.'

We crossed the square to the café. In my absence a few of the customers had been changed but the same transvestites (if such they were) were still parading in their pantherish fashion and, seeing us arrive, the fearfully mutilated cripples dispersed round the Square began to drag themselves or roll on their boards towards us.

The waiter brought thimblefuls of bitter coffee-substitute and a saucer containing seven sunflower seeds. To the right and left of us customers were moving draughts on their boards in a deliberate and stealthy fashion, and in absolute silence as if engaged in a conspiracy against the State. I got the impression that the Colonel was enjoying himself. He was the only man I had ever known whose eyes actually seemed to possess a life of their own, eluding the patrician control of his features to sparkle with pleasure and enthusiasm. The beggars had almost encircled us, edging their way nearer and nearer, gesticulating and mouthing entreaties, and something – perhaps self-discipline – permitted him, so far as I could see, utterly to ignore their presence.

'I imagine they continue to suffer from food shortages here,' he said.

'Inevitably,' I told him, 'with the end of the black market.'

'As you know,' he said, 'rationing drags on at home, but it's not too bad. Nobody goes short of anything. Having said that, it's extremely pleasant to get away for a break. I've started a little work project here to do with an exploration of the Byzantine mind as evidenced by spatial conceptions in art. I

166

could finish it in a month. If only the time lasts out, that's the trouble. If only I'm given the time.'

He was attracted by a last flush of light from below from over the edge of the mountain. By shifting our position a few yards we were given a view of the lowlands edged by the sea, where a deep green gloom had closed over the gardens, but great columns of mist wandered like phantoms, their tops in the sunset. A soft greenhouse scent of moving sap, water and night reached us at a thousand feet.

A harmless, smiling lunatic from the asylum down the hill led by a small boy attached to him by the thinnest of watch chains passed on his way back from his evening walk. The lights came on smearily in the square. The café radio had found a rumba, and the beggars shoved their angry faces closer to ours. I was waiting for some mention of the business that had brought the Colonel so urgently to Sicily, but he seemed in no hurry to turn to it. The customers had given up their games, and now they chewed sunflower seeds and spat. 'Why do they do that?' the Colonel asked. 'It's part of the day's routine,' I told him. '*U spassu*, the pastime. It's supposed to promote reflection.'

'A different world,' he said. 'More of India in it than Europe. There's a feeling in the air of resignation. Yet it's more positive than that. I fell under the influence of Sri Aurobindo while in Pondicherry. He taught that meditation and matter are linked. In India we adopted difficult postures to experiment with the mind. Here the chewing of sunflower seeds may suffice. What do you do here personally to pass time?'

'I record primitive music when I can find any. There's not much of it about any longer.'

'Fashions in most things change,' he said.

'They used to play a hydraulis up in a village near

167

Cammarata. An organ worked by water-pumps invented by the Greeks. By the time I heard about it they'd thrown it away. The radio took over.'

'I'd have been heart-broken,' he said. 'Lucky for me my interests lie in other directions.'

His expression suddenly sharpened.

'I got the feeling from your excellent report that the balloon might be about to go up.' This was an evident reference to the awaited separatist insurrection.

'I'm not sure about any balloon. The thing could die a natural death.'

'Really?' he said. 'So that's on the cards? This comes rather as a surprise. I seem to have read more into it than the facts warranted.' There was no mistaking his concern.

'Time isn't on our friends' side,' I said. 'The movement got under way through what was seen as a necessity to face a predicament. That predicament no longer exists.'

'But isn't there potentially a solid body of support among people of good will for a form of government prepared to say no to the squalid manoeuvrings of the past? A government offering in its place a philosophy of political regeneration plus the resurrection of the island's autonomous culture?'

'No,' I told him. 'Not in my opinion.'

'Why do you say that?'

'The Sicilians I know have their feet solidly planted on the ground. Tragic as it may seem, they can't afford the luxury of ideals. When I came back here three or four of my friends were firm separatists, but now I can't think of one who is. There's an election just round the corner; half the country is out of work and if you want a job it's better to vote DC. The Christian Democrats, known otherwise as the party of corruption, will get in.'

'But as you presented it to me the separatists refused to

168

play any part in the electoral farce, and who can blame them? They always made it clear that a trial of strength wasn't to be avoided.'

'But there's no strength any longer. Or whatever there was is fading fast.'

'When we spoke on the telephone I don't seem to recall you were so pessimistic about their chances?'

'I saved the pessimism for the sit-rep I sent off next day. Things at San Mauro are going downhill. There's no money and virtually no guns. The backers have faded away and the men who have to do the fighting would like to go home.'

Now with ultimate night the cripples had at last lost hope and dragged themselves away to leave us in peace, and the customers had ceased to chew their sunflower seeds and, stacking piles of minute coins on their tables, had abandoned their games, arisen as if moved by a common impulse and gone off. Men indistinguishable from Arabs were using palm fronds to sweep the square. A horse from *The Triumph of Death* drooped in the shafts of a spindly and ramshackle victoria. A single presumed transvestite strode away to be snatched up in the shadows cast from medieval walls. Suddenly the stolid, even grim outlines of the Cathedral came to life in incongruous, Christmassy fashion, as hundreds of small lamps festooning its walls were switched on. Once again we moved our chairs for a better view.

'I won't conceal from you,' the Colonel said, 'that my news, too, is a little depressing. Our superiors now take what they call a realistic view of the proposed involvement. Sicily would be expected in the long run to pay for whatever we have to offer, but it possesses nothing but sulphur and labour, of which the world has a glut.' He paused. 'I should tell you our American friends are here.'

'Back in Sicily again?'

'In Monreale. I've been talking to them. Their optimism remains undented. I expect you'll want to see them. I've forgotten the name of their hotel.'

'Rod and Nancy,' I said. 'A lively couple. I always suspected him of gun-running.'

'You may have been right. They seem exceptionally well-informed to be mere journalists. Nevertheless it could hardly have been more than a quixotic gesture.'

'I find Rod capable of cynicism.'

'It's a romantic posture American journalists adopt. Did you ever see *The Front Page*? It set a fashion.'

'Do you think the State Department could be involved in this?'

'What if they are, John? We've had our day, and they're surely entitled to their imperial dream. Did you uncover any evidence of significant support at San Mauro?'

'Only a few uniforms and several tons of powdered milk. Montelepre got some carbines but San Mauro's share of the handout seems to have been spirited away en route.'

'It's becoming a depressingly familiar story,' the Colonel said. 'Collapse, then, is inevitable?'

'As I see it.'

'And there's no chance of Giuliano coming down from the mountains?'

'It's unlikely.'

'What do you see happening now?' the Colonel asked.

'Whatever it is there was a snippet of information in yesterday's *Corriere* that suggested to me that things were moving fast.'

'Tell me about it.'

'It was nothing very much. Three lines on the back page squeezed in among the religious information. All it said was that the newly constituted 3rd Infantry Division of the

Italian Army was moving down from Trentino for routine exercises in the Sila, near Cosenza. Cosenza is thirty miles from the Straits. It could be in Sicily at any time now.'

'I live in hope that whatever you're led to deduce from this won't happen,' the Colonel said. 'We're threatened here with the loss of a last corner of the old unregenerate but delectable world. We shall never see its like again.'

The Colonel sighed, glanced at his watch and said he ought to be on his way. He was due to phone someone next morning, he said, at the incredible hour of eight – such was the zeal of those who were new to the game – and having disposed of this irksome obligation he proposed to come straight back, hunt down the amicable prebendary, and settle to a week's work in the Cathedral in the hope that he would be left in peace.

'I can see,' he said, 'I've so little time. So little time.' He asked me what my plans were, and offered me a bed in the office, but I explained that I was having a fault in the car's wiring fixed, and when it was ready I'd go down to Palermo and take a room in the Albergo Sole, where all the men of respect stayed because it was cheap and the service was good. It was left that I would phone him from Palma next evening, and with that he set off downhill in the office's old Fiat Millecento. When I went to pick up the car I found the job hadn't been done and wouldn't be finished that night, so there was nothing to do but stay in Monreale, and I booked in at the old Borgo.

This resounding palace of marble of many colours first acquired local fame when King Edward VII stayed there on one of his grand tours. His Majesty was known for his obsessive concern with the plumbing wherever he stayed, and the Borgo, warned in advance, had had a railway engineer design a lavatory especially for the occasion with a porphyry flush, lights under the seat, a built-in automatic waste-unblocking device and a musical box that played suitable tunes. This remained the pride and showpiece of the hotel, and was readily available for inspection by any visitor. What was no longer on view was the peep-hole in the wall of a room occupied by His Majesty through which he had been photographed while engaged with a lady of the town. I had been allowed on my previous visit, when Sicilians had been eager to please, to inspect the result which, although the monarch was recognizable, was much blurred through the time-exposure employed.

This time the new manager, smiling, tolerant, but perplexed, denied all knowledge of it.

'King Edward, sir? King Edward, yes sir. Come please.'

He ushered me up the steps of an enormously wide marble staircase, and into a room panelled by Lalique, with steps up to a tremendous throne. 'King Edward, sir,' the manager said. He pressed a button and Sicily's most famous w.c. thundered and chortled for my benefit, then we went downstairs.

The hotel was full of scurrying activity when I got up next morning. A very high staff–guest ratio is maintained in places of this kind, and everything in sight that could be polished was being polished, and small boys in uniform rushed to open doors, then went back to picking the withered leaves off potted trees. I took a quick turn in the Square, looked down into the green plain threaded with its bright rivulets, watched the straining lathered mules carrying the firewood up the hill, went back to the hotel, picked up a *Corriere* and made for the breakfast room.

It was tucked away at the back and I chose a table by an open window overlooking a Japanese garden created for the pleasure of the Archduke of Austria with a stream, bridge, pagoda and little, posturing trees. Waiters rushed in from two directions to shift place-settings and flick at non-existent crumbs, and at that moment there was a sudden, famished outcry from the rear: 'Hey, man what do you know. It's John,' and turning I saw Rod and Nancy at the next table.

I jumped up and went back to them, arms spread. We hugged each other like members of a close-knit family re-united after a long separation. Rod crushed my finger bones in a tremendous grip. Nancy wore her entrancing feminine version of a Pancho Villa smile as I kissed her on both cheeks. Rod bounced up and down with excitement, duck-ing suddenly, head down, to aim a series of fast, playful blows at my rib-cage, then, panting a little, began to shift the position of all objects within reach in an effort to burn up excess energy. 'What the hell are you doing here, man?' he asked. 'Isn't this something? We just got in from the States yesterday. Been back selling the pictures, and the magazines went for them in a big way. Sure, we're staying a week at least. Listen, you seen King Edward's jakes they have in this place? They tell me his inferiority complex was due to his cock being only four and a quarter inches long. I read some-where Queen Alexandra was a luetic with a hole in her head. Can you confirm that? For Christ-sake man, you're not eating. Grab one of these corn muffins. Want to know some-thing? Those muffins only started life at 6 a.m. yesterday the 16th in the Leibovitz Steam Bakery on 7th Avenue and 16th. We have a special relationship with the Airforce up here.'

In addition to the corn muffins and a variety of imported cereals the table was spread with all the accessories of a full-scale breakfast local style, much of it highly decorative; bas-kets filled with bread in the shapes of flowers and animals, chafing dishes of eggs and fritters, prosciutto cut and formed into hands, each holding a glistening black olive, and a cacciacavallo cheese of feudal proportions. A waiter came carrying a silver pot as reverently as a chalice on a tray, and poured a black flood into my cup. 'You can *drink* this coffee,' Rod assured me. 'We brought the beans with us. Notice the way that guy sniffed it. They haven't seen anything like that since the war began.'

'Tell me about the Giuliano trip,' I said. 'How did it go after I left?'

'It was great,' Nancy said. 'Wonderful. That's the only word for it. We knew we were onto something that was too big to leave. Listen, Rod and I can't thank you enough for the way you smoothed it for us. This turned out one of those world-exclusive things that don't happen any more. I mean we're in everything. *Nouvelles Images, Paris-Vie, Stern*. You name it. To say nothing about a double-page spread in *Life*. They really ate it up.'

'How about the shots of the execution?'

'Frankly in my view that was crap,' Nancy said. 'Sure we sold it around. But there was a similar thing from Guatemala *Life* ran at about the same time that put it into the back page.'

Rod said, 'This was a shambles. They had the guy sitting with his back to them in the end. It didn't read. There was nothing visual about it. Apart from that it was great. We went round with Giuliano for three days, and let no one tell you this is not a great man, because this is a guy with an extra dimension. You only have to speak with him and it kind of sinks in. Say, I hate to see you sit there and eat nothing. Have one of these blueberry pancakes.'

'So you got all the pictures you were after?' I said to Nancy.

'And more, many more.'

'Well, I'm glad of that. You went to a lot of trouble.'

'I filled a whole new portfolio. Crazy stuff. Really wild. Now we're looking for new worlds to conquer, hey, Rod? New worlds. My God John, it's great to see you again.'

Several bright little tousled children had found their way into the garden, come tripping and dancing over the humped-back bridge, encircled the porcelain pagoda and then arrived to inspect us through the window. Nancy, passing into the benign influence of the Indian god, gathered handfuls of muffins and pancakes and went out to feed them, and Rod followed her to scatter coins, which they collected somewhat doubtfully before taking their departure.

But no sooner had they gone than they were followed by the crippled beggars of the previous night hauling themselves painfully and noisily towards us through the ornamental trees. Their manner, as before, was angry and aggressive, and a waiter came padding up to shoo them away, but Nancy would have none of that. The Colonel would have dealt with this situation with a face in profile and utter withdrawal. Instead, Nancy asked in her most winning way for three clean bowls, *per favore, grazie*. They came and she filled them with assorted breakfast cereals, added sugar and milk, and then took them out, smiling graciously. The beggars ate without evident gratitude, then calmly and gently she got rid of them, using appropriate gestures. I was much impressed by the human, smiling fashion in which she pacified these poor, unfortunate creatures.

The incident was forgotten. Rod wanted to talk about the Cathedral. 'What an experience. We came up here as soon as we got in. Who do you think was the first person we saw? John Simmons, of all people. Some surprise.'

'Same thing happened to me,' I said. 'When I was told he was in Palermo I suspected that's where I'd find him. I know him of old.'

'He took us on a quick once-over of the place,' Rod said. 'Did you have any idea that the tableau showing Joseph wrestling with the angel contains 17,332 pieces of mosaic, the majority of them perfect squares? They estimate the building has subsided seven feet since construction was completed. Were you up on the roof? My God, is that a view.' He spluttered a little as he sometimes did, with enthusiasm, and pressed his napkin to his mouth.

'John's a mine of information on matters pertaining to culture,' Rod said. 'We were hoping to visit the Benedictine cloisters with him today. Can you imagine two hundred and sixteen columns and each and every capital different? John give you any idea how long he might be staying?'

'It all depends,' I told him. 'He's studying the local Byzantine art, so he wants to stay as long as he can. It's a matter of waiting to see which way the cat jumps.'

'We're in the same boat. You get this feeling of something in the air, and if it turns out to be big we have to be on the spot. Do you happen to know of a place called San Mauro? It's not on my map, but John said it was somewhere up in your neck of the woods.'

'It's not a town,' I told him, 'it's a mountain near Caltagirone. There's some trouble been going on up there for months. As far as I know the roads are closed.'

'The story is that that's where the action is, or will be,' Rod said. 'Is this some trip we could maybe make together if you happened to be able to spare the time?'

'I'd like to do it,' I said. 'Give me a day or two's warning if possible. You being a journalist I suppose they'd let us through.'

'There'd be no problem. We're given a big hand wherever we go.'

'Tell me frankly,' I said. 'Do you still believe the separatists have a hope in hell?'

'Of course we do.' A vibrant confidence bolstered Nancy's normally gentle and conciliatory tone of voice.

'It's much more than a hope, John, it's a certainty,' Rod said. 'For centuries Sicily has been subjected to alien rule. Now at last the Sicilians see the way open to them to make the break-away. These men are leading Sicilians towards their rightful place in the community of the free and democratic European nations. For this reason they're irresistible.'

18

Lo BIANCO RANG ME up at my office: 'In strictest confidence, could I bring a friend to see you? He has some interesting news.' Lo Bianco did not give his name but I recognized his voice. He preferred not to make a definite appointment, saying, we'll look in one evening in the hope you'll be about. I told him I went out most nights and that was how it was left. It was clear from the cautious approach that the friend was someone in deep trouble with the police.

They came the same evening a few minutes after I got back from the Square. Lo Bianco, shoving his friend ahead of him, ducked through the door as soon as it was opened, and even when inside the house continued to glance round in a nervous fashion, as if in fear of a bad surprise. The first thing I noticed was the extraordinary resemblance between Lo Bianco and his friend, although the friend was smaller and even slighter. Both men had young–old faces, fleshless and wasted, and suddenly I was reminded of Moscato's mummy from the catacombs, although the mummy's expression was less relaxed.

When we went up to the office both men, perhaps as a matter of habit, were careful to keep away from the windows, although there was absolutely nothing to be seen from the east-facing window but the division of darkness between sea and sky, while by crossing the room it was just possible to make out the black equilateral triangle of the volcano, the nearest light pricked into its flanks being some miles away.

I got off on the wrong foot. 'Is this man a bandit?' I asked Lo Bianco. The question slipped out, and was ill-advised. No one in this country would dream of admitting to being a bandit, any more than a man of honour would tolerate being referred to as a mafioso. Lo Bianco's friend, whose name was Turchino, meaning dark blue, spoke up for himself. 'I am a Niscemesi,' he said in a quiet voice, making it sound like a claim.

The Niscemesi were a feature of the mountains in the south-east, between Caltagirone and the coast, scattered groups of semi-outlaws who had been there so long that they had formed themselves into a clan system, spoke a semi-secret dialect full of outlandish words and had developed their own codes and a strict morality about which very little was known. They had lived long enough in isolation to have evolved strikingly different faces and minds from the islanders of the neighbouring villages and farms, and bore no resemblance to Giuliano's men who were shepherds who had fallen upon hard times and went in for a little banditry while waiting for things to look up. The Niscemesi were

179

tinkers and vets in the old gypsy style, always on the move, polyandrous – usually sharing a wife between two men – and augmenting their numbers by escapers from the sulphur mines who, after a period of probation, were admitted to their clans and given a share in a wife.

So this was one of them. So far as I knew I had never set eyes upon a member of this rare breed of man before, and studying him with curiosity and respect I was instantly aware of the mysterious impact of his personality. Turchino (it was the name of all the members of his clan – each clan being named after a colour) was not as other men, and I could understand the Niscemesi reputation for cunning, fearlessness and dignity, and the charm with which they disarmed their opponents, although it was said of them that they never smiled.

Lo Bianco said, 'I happen to be from Niscemi myself and no one's better in a position to assure you that banditry's an unknown evil in our part of the world. Can you tell me of any place of your knowledge where a woman can walk from one village to another through the mountains without fear of molestation? It doesn't exist. In Niscemi they press food on a stranger. Nobody will rob him. These people are Christians.'

In a most conciliatory and tentative way I asked Lo Bianco why he had thought it a good thing to suggest to Concetto Gallo, the Commander-in-Chief of San Mauro, that the bandits should be sent to do the requisitioning, rather than the gentlemen volunteers? To this he replied that there were Nescemesi in the camp, and there were bandits, and it was the bandits who had been sent after the Niscemesi had refused to be included in the requisitioning parties. 'Tell him how you and your friends came to be at San Mauro,' he said to Turchino.

180

Turchino, who had appeared uncomfortable in his chair, made this an excuse to get up. 'We're talking about people who live in mountains now. Just because nobody goes there it doesn't mean there's no owner. The owner gives us the right to graze our animals on his land. Even if he's never set eyes on it it's still his, and it is natural he should expect something in return. You're not in a position to pay him, but if he asks you to do something for him you do it. That's natural.'

'If you're looking for human gratitude,' Lo Bianco said, 'it exists here in its purest form.'

'In this particular instance the Baron Donnadolce allowed us to graze our sheep at San Mauro. He'd probably forgotten we existed, but never mind, some of us had been doing it for years, and nobody had given him so much as a kilo of cheese. One day a factor comes up to the summer pasture at Ramione, calls down the clan chiefs and says the Baron is having some trouble over his land, "which, by the way," he says, "is your land too, as you're the only ones who get anything out of it. He wants to know if he can count on your help?" We decided on the spot. He'd been good to us and we'd do what we could for him. We went down to San Mauro where they handed out guns, and each man had to sign his name on a paper with a cross in the presence of witnesses. We were told we were now members of a legally-constituted army, and that we would receive four hundred lire a day, and be free to go home at the end of the campaign.'

'Nobody understood what was meant by the word campaign, and nobody would tell them,' Lo Bianco said, 'the general impression up to this being that they were down there, as had happened in the past, to help the Baron with some problem over his boundaries with a neighbour. What really made them suspicious was that Gallo turned up and made a speech, telling them that they were fighting for freedom. These men aren't stupid. Freedom? they wanted to know. What freedom? It didn't make sense. They were about the freest people on the face of the earth as it was, so why should they fight for something they'd already got? And in any case, what had their freedom got to do with the Baron's boundary disputes? When they put this to Gallo he got nasty, and told them that he had proof that nearly every man among them was wanted by the police on one charge or another, and now by signing their names on the document they'd been given they'd committed an act of rebellion against the Italian State, and could expect prison sentences of up to fifteen years if they were captured by the Italians.'

It was a sad and typical story and was like a reading from history. This was the way, so far as those at the bottom were concerned, feudal societies must always have operated. In the civilizations of antiquity human surpluses requiring periodical clearing were usually created among the ruling class. The system devised by Norman ingenuity and logic worked the other way, producing a minimum of rulers who usually survived but an expendable excess of serfs. What astonished, once again, was the readiness of victims like Turchino to explain away, to excuse the tricks played upon them by those who manipulated their lives. The Baron had never realized what was happening behind his back. Someone had pulled the wool over his eyes. It was the factors and the stewards (themselves underdogs) who were to blame. And when things had been allowed to go a little too far, it was their heads that would be kicked around in a game of football while the 'unworldly' nobleman would be left in peace to the enjoyment of his revenues and his pursuit of the arts and sciences, with which such great men were accustomed to occupy themselves.

Turchino's story of his enlistment in the separatists held no surprise. It was a political cliché, a dodge used by Garibaldi and many other manipulators before and since his time of the anger and the innocence of the poor.

'How many of your people are there at San Mauro?' I asked Turchino.

'All the men of the three clans,' he said. 'Really, I don't know,' and I remembered that it was highly unlikely that he could count up to a hundred. 'You see the way we live means you have to be on the move all the time. The children have to be looked after and things have to be carried. We don't sleep two nights in the same place. We ask now to be allowed to go home to our families.'

'What's to stop you?' I asked. 'Tell them you've had enough of it, and go.'

'If we do that they say we're deserters. If they catch a deserter they hand him over to the police.'

'But they're against the police. They're fighting the police. How can they do that?'

'The Commander's done a deal with them. The police say they've found a man carrying a weapon, and they lock him up until they've got four more. It has to be five before they can charge you with banditry. As soon as they've collected five of us, that's it.'

I had to make a show of amazement, but such manoeuvrings, however labyrinthine, were commonplace. Everybody knew that the great men who headed or backed the separatists, conspirators and rebels that they were, were on excellent terms with the police, just as was the supreme bandit Giuliano himself, and the papers had published pictures of him and all the rest of them at festive and congratulatory gatherings with carabinieri colonels and chief inspectors of the Public Security in the best restaurants in towns within easy reach of the place where armed revolt was being prepared.

'The question is what if anything's to be done at this stage?' I asked. 'When you came here to see me you must have had something in mind.'

'We understand the soldiers are on their way. If there's any fighting we're the ones that will have to do it and if anyone gets killed apart from us they'll say it's murder.'

'What they're asking for is a general pardon,' Lo Bianco said. 'Some sort of amnesty. They're quite ready to lay down their arms and come out with their hands up in the air and that will be the end of the thing. So long as the slate's cleared.'

'But do you see that I can do anything for you?'

'We were hoping you could. When you asked me about the rebellion the other day, and I told you how it was in the camp, I got the feeling that you might feel inclined to put in a word for people who are kept in it through no fault of their own. If somebody could talk to the Duke –'

'I doubt if even the Duke could help in this case.'

'Or the Archbishop. What the Archbishop says goes.'

'He's up in the stratosphere as far as I'm concerned. I wouldn't even be put through to his secretary.'

'We're still Allies. What was the war about? You got rid of the fascists, and you cleared out the Germans. Surely you've got some say as to what goes on?'

'None at all,' I said. 'I'm a private citizen. A tourist. I'm here on sufferance. If I step out of line I'll be shown the door.'

'But you do see it's unfair?' he insisted.

'Yes,' I agreed with him, 'it's unfair,' and listening to him and pondering over the predicament this man's friends found themselves in, certain grim possibilities had occurred to me. San Mauro was very isolated. It was not to be found on any but the largest scale map. There was no town or substantial village within many miles. The narrow, winding roads that led to it had been sealed off. If ever there were a place out of the public's eye it was this. By this time, according to their claims, the separatists should have been in control of the province, but they were holed up in this valley – a dwindling and dispirited force with no armour, no artillery, obsolete rifles and machine guns, a shortage of ammunition, little food. Within days, a week or so at the most, the reformed and refitted infantry division with supporting artillery and tanks at present on manoeuvres in the Sila would move down to Reggio Calabria, slip across the straits and be on its way to San Mauro, for hardly more than what the divisional commander would see as an additional routine exercise.

Here – according to the official view – apart from the young political idealists who had flocked to the separatists' flag, were all the riff-raff of the mountains taken in a neat trap. Why investigators? Why big-scale trials (often accompanied by publicized scandals)? Why extra strain on the already over-stretched prison staff in maximum security gaols? Therefore why an amnesty when this situation could be dealt with so rapidly, so effectively, so discreetly and so conclusively by the forces of law and order?

Was there any court of appeal, any sympathetic ear that could be found? On the eve of the election and the formation of a government the area was full of shadow ministers, all of them tasting the sweetness of power devoid of the sour flavour of responsibility. 'The affair at San Mauro? Delighted to help if I could but I'm not your man. Scelba's tipped for the Interior. He's your best bet. In Rome at the moment. Why not give him a ring?'

'They'd never listen to me,' I told Lo Bianco. 'You can understand why. Until the day before yesterday most of them were separatists, but there's nothing going for them in that direction any longer. It's something they want to forget they've had any part of. They've their careers to think about. What can you expect?'

19

THE ARRIVAL IN PALMA of the first post-war reconstituted unit of the Italian regular army on its leisurely way southwards caused such excitement that the town council immediately ordered a festa in honour of San Rocco, most popular of local saints as patron of coitus interruptus and regular bowel movements.

Sicilians believed that semi-foreigners such as Italians were accustomed to a fairground atmosphere in celebrations of this kind, so a number of stalls were set up along the sea-front offering articles which were of little interest to the fresh-complexioned young soldiers from the industrial north. These included unusual sea-shells, St Agatha's breast-shaped cakes – the flavour of which for religious reasons was intentionally bitter – amulets in the shape of horns, 'relics' accompanied by outrageously forged certificates, pumpkin seeds, misty-looking photographs of the famous flying monk planing down from the sky with a wartime pilot in his arms, and a variety of panpipes and flutes upon which only the simplest pentatonic tunes could be played.

The soldiers found it hard to accept as fellow countrymen the small, furtive and ill-dressed Sicilians, with their ugly and incomprehensible dialect. Dressed in their new, green-dyed American uniforms, American bucket-helmets tilted rakishly over the left ear, with the fiercely-curled imperial moustaches of old worn again in the climate of awakening hope, they stood out head and shoulders from the lowly Sicilian crowd among which they strode with such confidence. The three thousand men of the New Model Army had not only been marched endlessly up and down barrack squares, and indoctrinated with the persuasive messages of democracy before being sent here, but virtually force-fed with Spam in response to a theory that this might foster a fighting spirit lacking according to some observers in Italian armies of the past.

Palma had been chosen as a rest area because it was the only town of any size before Caltagirone on the road to San Mauro. Backward, and dull, and smelling suspiciously of feudalism as the Italians found it, they were interested and in some cases cheered by the arrival of a busload of trans-vestites – another speciality of Catania along with play-wrights and clowns. Shortly, too, robust and mature Englishwomen from other parts of the island began to come on the scene in their familiar horse-drawn caravans, bring-ing with them their straps and whips. The soldiers were dis-mayed to find that nubile women in general were inaccessible; rarely even to be seen except on the rooftops, and ill-feeling was sometimes provoked by their habit of stationing themselves on the streets where the possibility arose of exciting themselves by looking up their skirts. All officers of the division were given honorary membership of one or another of the clubs in the Square, those of the rank of major and above being invited to watch the tedious routines of provincial life at the usual evening hour from behind the enormous window of the Civilized People's Club, while captains and below were accommodated among the spittoons of the Cultural Circle. Major General Giulio Césare Bertone, in command of the division, and members of his staff attended a reception in their honour given at the Town Hall by the scoundrelly-looking ex-lifer appointed Mayor by the Allies three years before. Here he was astonished by his encounter with Minasola who had driven in his 1929 Renault straight from his farm, smelling as strongly as ever of cow-dung, to clap him on the back and promise to look after him and his men while they were on his, Minasola's, home ground in every way he could. The general was mollified to be told that Minasola, despite his appearance and odour, was the town's leading citizen and that he had treated the German area-commander in his time in exactly the same way.

The presence of the army provided a much needed boost to the economy of the town. There was practically no money in circulation, and the barter system had re-asserted itself to such an extent that it was not extraordinary for a patron of the Roma to arrive in the morning with some small household article or even a bunch of carrots from his garden, to be used in payment for the day's intake of coffee-substitute. The soldier's eternal problem, however poorly he may be paid, is to find ways of getting rid of money accumulated

189

over the periods when there is nothing whatever in sight on which it can be spent. In a matter of days they emptied the taverns of their stock of the deplorable wine of the region, and then stuffed their kitbags with such things as cheap alarm-clocks and mirrors encrusted with sea-shells, which were the only souvenirs Palma produced.

Both Crispi and Moscato had experienced unexpected upswings in their fortunes. Someone told General Bertone about Crispi's renown as a producer of genealogical charts, and the general, scion of a successful family of shoe-manufacturers, showed interest in tracing back his ancestry. 'I had to explain to him that I only provided Sicilian ancestors,' Crispi said. 'And he said that didn't matter.' Crispi was fully installed in the surviving half of the post-office now ('I've ditched the widow for good and all'), working in the large room where a few days previously the recent staff had been selling stamps and postal orders across the counter before grabbing up hats and handbags to make a run for it. With the orders flowing in he was almost into mass production. 'I told the General he might as well go for the Swabians,' he said, 'and he agreed. After all, he could afford it.' The junior officers with not too much in the kitty had been put on to the Risorgimento of 1845 as a special inducement at two thousand lire a kick.

Moscato did a bumper trade with soldiers who, wandering into the museum because they had nowhere to go, were entranced by its macabre assistant dancing with the Johnny Walker from the Palermo catacombs. After that they happily plonked down ten lire for Moscato's hair-raising lecture on murder by flesh-consuming injection as illustrated by the victims of the mad Prince of Sanseverino's experiments, reduced to the bagfuls of blood vessels and bones hanging in his cupboard.

Economic gains apart, there were certain drawbacks inherent in the situation of a small and backward town suddenly called upon to play host to a large number of soldiers. Palma males of an equivalent age were poor and hungry, whereas by Sicilian standards members of the Italian armed forces were affluent in the extreme and designedly over-fed. Italian soldiers of the reconstituted division strutted in the Corso stuffed with processed pork, jostling civilians and on the avid watch for feminine buttocks to pinch. Once in a while they actually carried out this feat, but reaction was inevitable, and several of them, enticed away into shadowy places, were stabbed with almost surgical precision, leaving a trifling wound hardly more than an inch in depth. The knife went in and out before the soldiers so much as glimpsed it. Murder was not intended, only a final warning. Bottom-pinching came to an end.

'Wartime parties are always better,' Moscato said. 'Life seems shorter and sweeter. There's more excuse to kick over the traces. Not that you can call this a war. It'll be finished within a couple of days, but it's better than nothing.'

I was on my way with Moscato and Crispi to a reception for the officers of the Italian Army at the Prizzi Palace, which with immense energy and devotion had been smartened up for the occasion and stuffed with furniture of all descriptions and from a number of sources. The Bianchi had broken down once again, and since it was impossible, as Moscato had assured me, to arrive on foot, we had taken a spindly carriage of a kind known as a *milord*, drawn by a horse reduced by starvation to a slow but dignified walk.

The night air was like warm milk and full of insects, chased by innumerable bats. A trio of drunken privates went reeling down the street on the look-out for trouble, and

Moscato gazed after them with affection. 'The best parties were held during the wonderful days of the First World War,' he said.

'I was just out of school,' Crispi said. 'I can remember them. But no more than that.'

'To really enjoy a war,' Moscato said, 'you have to be as far from the action as possible, and of course on the winning side. Given those two essentials the experience is incomparable. We were spellbound. One picked up the excitement like a sickness and passed it on. Wild affairs on all sides. I was lightly wounded in a duel myself.'

'Rubbish,' Crispi said. 'You're making it up.'

'You wouldn't understand,' Moscato said. 'Those days are gone, never to return.'

'They never existed outside your imagination,' Crispi said. 'How did you enjoy the Abyssinian War, or were you out of favour by that time?'

'The answer to your question is that I enjoyed it enormously, and my fall from grace took place a year after it was all over. Once again I recall a series of glittering occasions. Surely even you must have had a good time at the Victory Ball at the Gallieni Palace? I know you were there.'

'Actually I did,' Crispi said. 'It was the first and last time I danced with the Marchesina and she even went to my head. She was in great demand in those days, with all the captains and majors after her.'

'But when it came down to brass tacks, no takers even then. A man wants to marry a woman, not a circus turn. Did you know that the Conte Gallieni had been captured and castrated in the Ogaden?'

'I heard a rumour to that effect,' Crispi said.

'I can speak with authority on the subject as he discussed the matter quite openly with me, and with a good deal of spirit. He'd undergone his unfortunate experience some months before we met. He said he'd always considered his testicles a bit of a nuisance and didn't really mind being parted from them. As you know, he was a keen music lover, and he told me he'd noticed a heightening in his artistic appreciation in general besides an increase in his singing range by a note or two – although not so much as he would have hoped for.'

'He was always very enthusiastic about the Germans,' Crispi said.

'I thoroughly enjoyed having them with us too,' Moscato said. 'Who didn't? We rather liked the British as well, even if they were the biggest thieves in history. Fortunately the American allies only interested themselves in what they used to call pussy and liquor.'

Moscato, Crispi and I, plus a few chosen members of the Civilized People's Club, found a concentration of unattached males at the bottom end of the long table, while the Marchesina and her neighbours from the adjoining palaces were engaged with the General and his officers at the top. The organizers of the party had clubbed together to engage six well-mannered prostitutes from a specialist house in Catania, not necessarily for any direct sexual activity but in the manner of Japanese geishas, to keep the party going. It was an accepted fiction that they should have been represented to the guests as local girls of good family for whom the Marchesina acted as chaperone. Fishermen's wives offering their services free out of a sense of feudal obligation served at table dressed in folk costumes from the museum once worn by members of an Albanian colony in a different part of the island. The Seaweed Eater, similarly attired, rushed past at frequent intervals laden with containers of water on her way to the loft to keep the fountain running. It had been decided among the organizers that a medieval atmosphere should be fostered. The weak and intermittent electricity supply was therefore supported by the smeary flames of a number of rush tapers that had been made up with some difficulty, and the fact that visibility remained extremely poor was seen as all to the good.

'Look at the way they eat,' Moscato said, watching the officers bent over their plates. 'Imagine Spam twice a day, seven days a week. It's not to be wondered at.'

'What did you say this has been passed off as?' Crispi asked.

'Wild boar,' Moscato said. 'Unfortunately they don't exist in this part of the island. I'll tell you the real story when you've finished.'

'There wasn't enough of anything to go round,' Moscato explained to me, 'so the museum was approached to help out in various ways. Some of the objects they've put on display seem grotesque to me, but our guests appear to be impressed so what does it matter?'

The courtyard had been converted hastily into a species of banqueting hall relying heavily on patched tapestries and murky paintings of religious subjects. The Samurai in armour was back, and someone had lent a stuffed horse ridden by Garibaldi in his campaign, called Vercingetorix by the General, who had always admired the French. The usual collection of spurious blunderbuses and horse pistols were suspended over the wall-hangings. There were several supposedly fifteenth-century *cassoni* painted with atrocious scenes of battle. The museum had supplied an Etruscan vase depicting a warrior with an impossible phallus. One palace had provided a case of seventeen birds of paradise, their plumage gnawed away to the skin by generations of red mites. Another's prize possession on show here was a vast tableau of the *Titanic* to which an extra funnel had been added, foundering among the icebergs in a sea of glass. Several of the Marchesina's neighbours had brought patrician dogs along, including a pair of relentlessly flatulent Azerbaijanian deer hounds.

'Naturally they're impressed,' Moscato said. 'Why shouldn't they be? These are shopkeepers' sons from places like Turin which consists largely of cement works and tyre factories. They've heard a lot about Sicilian feudalism, and here it is, and they love it. How are they to know the council just served a notice on Count Gallieni to shore up his palace properly or they would knock it down?'

'Now I've finished the wild boar,' Crispi said, 'do you mind telling me what it was?'

'Plain straightforward pig,' Moscato said. 'One that died a natural death. Hog cholera. There's a lot of it about.'

'How do you know?'

'Because I was asked to inspect the cadaver.'

'But was it fit for human consumption?'

'Just,' Moscato said.

'But it's not dangerous?'

'No, only disgusting.'

'I'm thankful you didn't tell me,' Crispi said.

'How did you find it, John?' Moscato asked me.

'Delicious. A trifle gamey perhaps.'

'The real thing is gamier. Have some more, I'm going to.'

I drained my glass, noticing instantly a slight pounding in the right temple. 'What by the way are we drinking?' I asked.

'Nominally Montibello-Clássico,' Moscato said. 'A connoisseur's choice from a local vineyard of limited production. Actually among friends we call this barrel-washings, fortified in this case with a little of my pickling spirit. I'd recommend you to stick to one glass.'

'Perhaps the guests should have been warned,' Crispi said.

But it was too late. In the developing uproar voices were heard calling for music. The pseudo-Albanian servitors were clearing a space. A gramophone had been produced, a record put on, and the dancing began. The music had been provided by the Army. In Palma di Cava on the rare occasions when dances were held the foxtrot was still considered an innovation, but the north of Italy had moved rapidly with the times into the era of the conga, which called for a total subservience to simple rhythm and practically no skill. Within a matter of minutes a demonstration had been given and the line formed with the Marchesina strutting and cavorting at its head. It curved and coiled like an intoxicated serpent under the guttering rushlights, round the long table with its tipped-over glasses, past the posturing Samurai, the defeathered birds of paradise in their case, the sinking *Titanic* and Garibaldi's stuffed horse. The maracas rattled, the drums thudded and the Marchesina uttered little ecstatic shrieks at the handsome staff-captain, young enough to have been her son, following her in the line, puddling at her hips.

I joined in at the tail end with Moscato and Crispi and the scrawny dowagers and mad old geriatrics covered with fascist decorations who believed Mussolini was still alive. But both men had slender reserves of energy to draw upon, and after a while we gave up and sat down again.

The Marchesina and her staff-captain came jerking past again, and Moscato shook his head. 'Drunk as a skunk,' he said. 'I'm referring to him, not her, of course, ever. At this moment she probably looks like a fairy princess to him, and to tell the truth she does to me. On the other hand I must admit it exhausts me just to look at her. I see you've rather faded out of the picture.'

'It's something I accept,' I said. 'She usually manages to get a boyfriend out of a party. The trouble is armies are always on the move.'

'This has been turned into a palace of illusions,' Moscato said. 'Nothing is what it seems to be. The Marchesina's got herself up to look like a young girl's first response to the call of love, whereas to my certain knowledge she's been operated on three times for the restoration of virginity. The pictures are all copies, and the tapestries are fakes. Apart from the Marchesina the only pretty women in the room are prostitutes, passed off as the daughters of noble families, specializing, as they tell me, in fellatio, much practised by the ancients but subsequently out of fashion until brought back by our American friends. As an example of something that goes right to the heart of the farce I draw your attention to the amazing spectacle of my old friend Count Gallieni, damaged in the way we know him to be, groping one of them in the corner over there. Do you fancy any of our Catania scrubbers, Crispi?'

'All of them,' Crispi said.

'And so do I,' Moscato said. 'Just to watch them strips the years away.'

'I'm letting my imagination run riot,' Crispi said. His eyes were brighter, even his flabby, wrinkled cheeks seemed to have firmed up.

'But it's an illusion,' Moscato said. 'All an illusion.' He turned to me. 'Like most of my friends I've read Shakespeare through from end to end, but there's not a single one of his glorious lines I can quote accurately. He says something about our being no more than the substance of dreams. Do you remember the passage, Crispi?'

'I know how it goes on,' Crispi said. '"And our little life is rounded by a sleep."'

'And that's true also, that's true,' Moscato said. 'So let's make the most of it, illusion or not. The real question is, are you enjoying yourself?'

'I am,' Crispi said. 'It's been a good party even by the old standards. Noisier, but none the worse for that.'

'And thus,' Moscato said, 'we say goodbye to feudalism. From now on we'll have to learn to be realists. I expect we'll get used to it.'

20

THE PROSPECT OF AN approaching conflict that could be presented to the reading public as something hardly short of civil war was a godsend for newspapers in the doldrums of summer. This was a time when it was said that even the saints in the churches could be heard groaning with boredom, and with people tending to take time off from life fall into a coma, newspaper circulation slumped practically to nothing. At least a hundred pressmen descended upon Palma and so far from being exclusively paparazzi who made up the news as they went along, a number were journalists of reputation sent by such prestigious mainland papers as *Il Tempo*. These, having settled hopefully with their typewriters in such squalid accommodation as that offered by the

Roma, found little to fill the column inches while awaiting the hard news. Surely something has to happen once in a while, even in a place like this, protested the men from Genoa and Roma. It did, but they had come on the scene too late. A month or two earlier there had been news stories in plenty. Miners had gone on strike and been dealt with in the customary way. Peasants had been convinced at last of the infeasibility of attempting to occupy uncultivated land, and here as elsewhere people like Miraglia, ignoring the customary warnings to stop causing trouble, had gone the way of all flesh. Now a stagnant version of peace had returned. The Palma news agency offered a few lackadaisical suggestions for those who felt compelled to file copy at all costs. Mention was made of the 'truth festa' at a local shrine where all those who attended were under traditional obligation to speak out their innermost thoughts about the friends accompanying them – a release of inhibitions that had once provoked affrays in plenty. Apart from this, writers short of material were invited to interview a woman of feeble intellect, aged 113, who in her whole life had never allowed food other than ricotta and whey to pass her lips, or a deserter from the First World War who shared a cave with a bear and had lost the power of speech.

Encouraged by the lethargy of his colleagues, Signorelli, the *Il Tempo* man, decided to try for a scoop and found some way of brazening his way into the separatists' headquarters at San Mauro. Some news of his adventures filtered through before they appeared in print and I rang him up and went to see him at the Roma. I found him in a room full of whining mosquitoes, into which five beds had been crammed. We sat on the edge of a bed under a mosquito net for a moment, then he suddenly jumped to his feet, tore the net to shreds and we adjourned to the dining room to discuss matters as best we could among the outcry of the scopa players and well within range of the cow's intestines being cleaned out for the evening meal. He was old and untidy, professionally hard-bitten, with a stock-in-trade of shallow anger and an immense detestation for the Sicilian scene.

'I was picked up and taken to Gallo's tent,' he said. 'I took one look at the man and said to myself, this is a maniac. Out of touch with reality. He wanted me to have dinner with him. Two kinds of wine, pâté de foie gras, baby lamb with all the trimmings, brandy to follow. Imagine that.' He looked at me sternly. 'What would your impression have been?'

'That he wanted you to believe there was no shortage of food.'

'Right. Exactly that.' Suddenly he went red in the face. 'Listen, I can't think with that row going on.' He got up waving his arms about and went across to the scopa players. The noise subsided and he came back and fell into his chair again, a little short of breath like a man out of condition who'd run a short race to catch the bus.

'When a general or a politician invites me for a meal I ask myself what's at the back of it? What does this man want of me? They had soldiers running up and down all the time, and a tank going round in circles. But why? That was the question I asked myself. What's all the show in aid of? How would you have felt about it all?'

'Suspicious, possibly.'

'Inevitably. Just as I was. Gallo took me up the side of the mountain and said, "Do you see those guns?" There was something poking out of the mountainside that could have been guns, or equally well it could have been tree-trunks. It was impossible to tell at that distance. "One-o-five howitzers," he said. Do you think I'm mad? I wanted to say. "The heavy stuff," he said. "We have a few one-three-fives, too," he told me, "but we keep them under cover. The mountain is honeycombed with tunnels. This is a Maginot Line in miniature, although our spirit here is very different from that of the French of those days." While he was giving me all this bull the same tank kept going round the camp with a fellow looking like a skeleton in uniform standing up in the turret. They were all of them as thin as rakes. All the men I saw seemed to suffer from skin trouble. Their skin was cracked and reddened. Could that have been pellagra?'

'It probably was.'

'Generals and politicians,' Signorelli said. 'This is the kind of line you can always expect them to take, and I'm so tired of it. If Gallo hadn't wanted to use me it would have been bean stew in the sergeant's mess for dinner.'

'By the sound of it you don't hold out much hope for our friends.'

'I don't hold out any hope at all.'

'Did you know that most of them want to give up, but Bertone won't let them?'

'Why should he? Generals are in the murder business. Of course he won't let them surrender.'

The more thought I gave the journalist's story, the more I was convinced that, as he himself suspected, his experiences at San Mauro as a guest of Concetto Gallo had been stage-managed with some energy and a fair degree of skill. This conclusion in its turn disposed of a lurking doubt that Lo Bianco and Turchino might have been plants schooled in a story of doom and despair to be spread as part of a plan to induce the government forces to under-rate the strength and preparedness of the rebels. My view now was that the situation was just as Lo Bianco had described it, although it was a little hard to see what Gallo hoped to gain by the charade unless it was to persuade General Bertone to call off the attack. Since then Turchino, it seemed, had slipped away back to San Mauro, but Lo Bianco had been arrested on a charge of conspiracy to foster rebellion and held for some days before managing to talk himself out of his predicament. Following his release he was besieged by reporters who published a number of accounts of life in the camp of San Mauro they claimed he had given them, although most of them were stolen from Giovanni Verga and other writers on the ancient disasters of Sicily.

General Bertone, now renamed General Baggéo (Bugger-all) by the newsmen, continued to regard Lo Bianco's story with distrust. A helicopter was procured in Rome, dismantled, transported by rail to Sicily, reassembled and then took to the air to photograph the San Mauro area, returning in due course with several hundred pictures of the wrong mountain. Following this fiasco – the helicopter could not be persuaded to take off a second time – a Niscemesi serving a long sentence in the Ucciardone prison in Palermo was offered a pardon if he would agree to go to San Mauro and act as spy. He was released and brought to Palma and his son aged fourteen was taken from the family home and brought to the camp to be held as hostage for his father's return. The boy dug himself out of the hut they'd put him in, and the father knocked an officer off his horse and escaped.

These two reverses may have influenced Bertone's tactics. It was announced that by the latest estimates there were five thousand rebels entrenched at San Mauro, and he sent for reinforcements from the mainland – particularly artillery and tanks. While these were on the way, Bertoni moved a force of two thousand assault troops to surround the area and prepare for the attack. These designs and plans, with much fictitious addition, were duly announced in the press.

Next day half the roads in Palma were closed and the traffic diverted to allow the passage through the town of the tank transporter and self-propelled guns. The last of the infantry moved out and the army had gone, leaving little to show of its presence but discarded tyres, empty oil drums and rolls of abandoned barbed wire. Its departure was followed by that of all the pressmen who could arrange transport for themselves, the transvestites from Catania travelling by bus, and a slow procession of Englishwomen in their caravans, who hoped to catch up with the army in Caltagirone. This left Palma free to relapse into its midsummer trance.

I had settled to spend an hour shifting the positions of the outstanding claims in the file when the phone rang and the Colonel was on the line from Palermo. 'I hear something may be about to happen at San Mauro,' he said.

'At long last,' I said. 'Whatever happens, the result's a foregone conclusion. It's only a matter of days.'

'Are you so sure of that?'

'I was never surer of anything.'

'The reports coming in here are somewhat confused. Would there be any chance of your going down there and putting me in the picture as to what's going on?'

'It may be difficult,' I told him, 'but I'll do what I can.'

I rushed back to the Roma in the hope of catching an Italian journalist there who might be able to suggest a way of getting through to San Mauro, half-convinced in advance that the thing was impossible. Then I saw the Steins' enormous Dodge parked outside the hotel's entrance in the square, and my hopes slightly revived.

Rod and Nancy were in the dining room in conference as I came in with Giovanni, the old waiter. Once again I was struck by their dynamism, by their presence, their glamour, the vivacity of their gestures, even their sheer size in this environment of glum looks, sallow light, murky odours, stained napery and pigmy humanity. A large container of US Forces refined sugar, the gold of the day, stood with Giovanni cringing before it on the table, signifying that a barter deal was in the offing. My two American friends looked up and saw me, leaped from their chairs and we embraced.

'You're in time after all,' I said. 'Quite thought you'd never make it.'

'Well we did and we didn't, John,' Rod said. 'It was a nice excuse to drive halfway round the island to see you, but as it turns out this is the end of the road. I guess in more ways than one.'

'You mean you're not going on to San Mauro?'

'We ran into difficulties,' Nancy said. 'Seems we need a laisser-passer and we don't have one, so it stops here.'

'But you're press.'

'American press. Maybe we're out of favour,' she said.

'I can't believe that. There must be something we can do. Do you want me to call the Colonel? He may be able to pull strings.'

'That's nice of you John, and I appreciate it. This is going to come as a surprise, but while Nancy and I have been sitting here we've reached a decision. What we propose to do is to have a pleasant and relaxed meal in which we much hope you'll join us, and right after that we're going to get into that car outside, turn round, and go back. We're pulling out.'

'But why? Wasn't this going to be the great scoop of all time?'

'No one can get a scoop out of what's happening here.'

205

'What about *Life* and the *Tribune*. Surely they're still interested?'

'This is what we describe in the trade as a fadeout. When I called the *Tribune* office this morning I spoke to a man who practically yawned into the phone. The time we first came down here there was some crazy talk going round about turning this into the forty-ninth State. Naturally they were interested. Well, it hasn't happened that way and they want to be allowed to forget it. The *Tribune* can use three hundred words on San Mauro to go in facing the sports page. *Life* cabled Nancy, "exclude Gallo Giuliano further reportage". They seemed to think both guys were the same man.'

'What do you put this down to?'

'Loss of interest,' Rod said. 'The reading public is looking elsewhere for its kicks. There's a big story in Berlin. Things are happening in the Far East. Giuliano was a shooting star that fell to earth. He gave us a nice run and now it's over. Otherwise, what does Sicily have to offer? Temples, guys knocking each other off, big funerals. This place is a hollow laugh. Reluctantly or otherwise, we have to be where the action is.'

'It always seemed to me it was more than a job of mere reporting you were doing on Giuliano. I got the impression of a personal involvement.'

'There was,' Nancy said. 'Almost. But by the very nature of this profession involvement can only be a temporary thing. I guess you could even describe us as emotional nomads. Whatever we're into we give it all we've got, but when the time comes to move on we cut the lifeline. Rod and I have a word for this. We call it positive re-alignment. That is our professional philosophy. When you walk away from the scene you don't look back.'

I nodded understandingly, wishing in a way that it was a philosophy I had been able to adopt at a much earlier period in my life, which had remained so backward-looking, so overcast by memory. 'And you have no regrets?' I had once asked Rod wonderingly, and he seemed surprised as though the question had to do with masturbation rather than sorrow. 'Hell, no,' he assured me. 'Nancy and I use a plan that takes care of that. In the Bab movement I was telling you about they issue a viva-print tailored to suit your particular case. Stick to the rules and the annual balance sheet comes out right every year. We don't regard this as a religion because stuff like worship and prayers are out, but you could see it as a business arrangement with God.'

Nothing could have been more agreeable than to spend the rest of the day with the Steins, trying to delve further into the sources of their inner strength, but at this point our meeting was disrupted by the surprise reappearance of Signorelli from *Il Tempo* who came limping into the room bellowing rage and frustration at his predicament. His car had let him down and he had kicked it so hard that he had probably broken a toe, and had come here hoping to find someone to give him a lift. I offered to take him in the Bianchi if he could guarantee to get us through and he said there would be no difficulty about that.

I said goodbye to Rod and Nancy, and we assured each other that sooner or later we should meet again in some troubled and defenceless country where such special qualifications as we were supposed to possess were most likely to be in demand. Five minutes later Signorelli and I were on our way to San Mauro.

My friend was one of those old newspaper men who have settled down comfortably with their paranoia and are full of complaints. At the hotel they had mixed the coffee he had brought from Rome with acorns; he had found a duck's foot in his stew, and his toe was so swollen he had to take off his shoe. 'How long will this take?' he asked. 'This car was built for dwarves. I'm getting cramp in the arse.'

There was a checkpoint a few miles down the road. Here among a great snarl-up of traffic the transvestites' bus had been held up and was about to be turned back, and what would have appeared to an outsider as a bus-load of beautiful and elegantly turned-out women were baying their fury at the police in baritone voices and an unmistakably masculine fashion.

An officer, his cheeks pink-flushed with his diet of spiced pork, asked to see our papers, then waved us on; the transvestites' outcry died away in the rear, and we were on our way to Caltagirone, catching no more than a faint whiff of the sheep's turds for which this city is celebrated as we bypassed its centre to drive along ever-narrowing roads into the bare, wild country beyond. Even in these backwoods we were much held up by military vehicles which had clearly taken wrong turnings and lost their way, and having brought a large-scale map with me I left the main road shortly after Caltagirone, and we began to work our way using cart-tracks across country, arriving shortly at a village called Cattara only a few miles from San Mauro.

Twenty or so countrymen in striped flannel shirts and enormous flat hats sat outside the village bar in a kind of moody, concentrated silence, their eyes fixed on the carcase of a horse suspended from a hook in the butcher's across the road. Apart from the head and legs which had been left as in life, the carcase had been flayed, and the butcher was rotating it very slowly on the hook as if to display its points to potential customers.

This was the old, obsidian, basic Sicily where no questions were in any circumstances asked, where they didn't even play noisy card games and no one had much to say, and there was a hush in the atmosphere that could almost be felt. We assumed that the action against San Mauro would begin at dawn, according to tradition, and agreed to try to spend the night here. I asked for the man of respect and one of the countrymen sitting outside the bar got up and introduced himself with a kind of withdrawn affability. I explained what was wanted and he assured us that it gave him huge pleasure to be able to help in any way. He took us to a small saturnine building consisting of a single room with a loft, and giving the impression that it had been unoccupied for some years. The door, provided with a speakeasy flap, must have been four inches thick, and although there were no windows, slits had been left in the walls, through which I supposed a gun could have been fired if necessary. As in Russia of old, one slept in winter on top of a large, brick stove. The man of respect smiled bleakly. 'No one will trouble you here,' he said.

What was curious, and yet perhaps in a way typical of men such as my friend, was that the prospect of a night spent in the fetid darkness of this mosquito-ridden cavern did not daunt him in the slightest. If anything, the reverse. He hummed a bar or two from some Italian opera, slapped me on the back, and said, 'Let's go and eat.' We went back to the bar, consumed a platter of horse apiece cut from the carcase still hanging from the hook, and drank a litre of black wine tasting of earth, which my friend found 'unusual' but was happy to tolerate. He liked the people of Cattara, all of whom through interbreeding looked almost exactly alike. 'Genuine,' he said. 'Quite unspoilt. Do what they can for you, and say what they think.' We went back to the house.

'It's like a furnace in there,' he said, 'but in case you don't know I'll show you how to cope with the situation.'

There was a well outside the door, and we threw buckets of water over each other, and then lay down on the stove top in our wet clothes. Minutes later I was asleep.

Next morning the man of respect was waiting for us outside soon after four. It was the best time of the day, with the blackbirds singing and the great hump of San Mauro coming up out of the mist with a view of gorges and precipices and great gnarled and twisted pines of the kind drawn by Chinese painters of the old school clinging to the slopes. We told the man of respect that we wanted to watch the battle and he agreed that it could be an interesting sight. He offered to take us to a better vantage point and we were on our way to this when we saw a police van with barred windows guarded by two carabinieri parked near the bar. At the moment of our arrival several young men in tattered uniforms escorted by more carabinieri came up a path, and were put in the van. I noticed that two of them were weeping. My friend went over to try to talk to the young men, but they hustled them away. The man of respect said that these were separatist volunteers who had given themselves up and were being taken in by the police.

'The story was there was no question of anyone being allowed to surrender,' I said.

'I only know what I'm told,' he said.

We followed him up the track and sat down on the trunk of a fallen tree that was being systematically devoured by termites. Some distant shooting was going on, but it came in sporadic bursts, and the sound of it echoing in the shallow basin of hills surrounding the mountain of San Mauro could at first have been taken for no more than a larger-than-average hunting party banging away at deer. Crows came up out of the woods, wheeled away in disordered formation and flew off in different directions, but otherwise there were no signs of life. Signorelli had been studying the map. 'Any idea where the separatists are likely to be?' I asked him.

He threw out his arm in a wide gesture that took in bluffs and escarpments, a low precipice, the thread of a waterfall, and tightly-grouped stands of trees. 'Anywhere up there. Take your choice. What does it matter?' He laughed in his usual mock-wrathful way.

'Anyway, we've certainly a ringside view.'

'Of what?' he said. 'What do you expect to see?'

The desultory firing became more regular and intense. I could pick out the slow stutter of the old heavy machine guns the Italians still used among the crackling of rifle fire.

'They fire at nothing,' Signorelli said, 'and always have done. Hundreds and hundreds of bullets fired at nothing, to keep their spirits up. I can imagine what's going on down there. They're kissing each other and handing out keepsakes and last messages for friends. Little do they know.'

I was about to ask him what he meant by the last remark when the big guns opened up. They were firing from dense cover in the valley about a mile to the left of us with what sounded like Örlikons normally used against aircraft, firing tracers and small calibre shells into the top of the mountain, and mixed in with their snap and yelp I heard the deep throaty cough of one of the eighty-eights the Germans had left behind, and the occasional stunning crack of an American howitzer that reminded me of the sharp, echo-less splitting of the deep ice in a lake in a sudden thaw.

'They bring the guns all the way from Italy,' Signorelli said, 'so they have to fire them. Every time they fire a one-three-o howitzer it's five million lire. After ten rounds they change the barrel. Every general has one to show his friends.' He grumbled on until the roar of the barrage swept over whatever it was he had to say and carried it away.

I felt a light tap on my shoulder. The man of respect stood there, his jacket collar turned up as if in expectation of rain. He took the tips of our fingers in his, bowed slightly, turned back down the path and disappeared from sight. Signorelli laughed again. 'I wonder if he imagines we're under fire?' he shouted to me.

Rockets ribboned from behind the trees to fall on an unseen target and a cluster of big, slow mortar bombs dragged their comets' tails of smoke across the sky. 'The only risk we run,' Signorelli said, 'is being shelled by our own valorous artillery, and that is far from slight.' At that moment, in fact, the earth shuddered as a howitzer shell exploded in the valley below, some quarter of a mile from the mountain's base.

An old blunt-nosed American fighter-bomber pushed itself over the shoulder of a hill, and came down the valley a few hundred feet above us, balancing itself, wings rising and falling, like a tightrope performer on the air currents. It dipped over the mountain and swung away, seemingly almost caught in an uprush of black vapours with fire flickering in the woods at their base. 'Incendiaries – possibly napalm,' Signorelli said. 'Mission accomplished. The grand finale.'

He was brimful of cantankerous glee. 'Ready then?' he asked. 'If we get out now we'll avoid the rush.' He made a pretence of surprise that I should be surprised. 'Are you taken in by all this?' he asked.

'I don't quite understand.'

'Surely you realize that all this is a fraud? This is a show put on to make them feel happy back in Rome.'

'I can't believe that.'

212

'Believe what you like. They went in yesterday and found the birds had flown. The general had to win a battle and this is it. People in the know say that when they found the caves were empty they took a few old gaolbirds up there and put them in so that the photographers would have some corpses to show for their pains when it was all over.'

We were shouting at each other in the lulls in the racket. He was enjoying himself, and full of savage laughter.

'In that case, what was the point of your coming up here?'

'I had to produce some sort of story.'

'Wouldn't it make a sensation in this particular case if you wrote the truth?'

'It would,' he said, 'but I'm too old to find another job.'

I was facing him with my back to the mountain and he had changed colour as if he were looking into a sunset. Turning, I saw the whole of the mountain-top crested with fire. A wind blowing towards us carried grey flakes of ash that were lighter than snow.

'We may as well go,' I said.

21

THE ROAD BACK TO Palma was clear. I dropped Signorelli off at the telegraph office to get his piece on the wire, then telephoned the Colonel.

'I managed to get through almost to San Mauro, and saw what little there was to be seen. In theory the battle's still raging, or it was a couple of hours ago, but I think we can say it's all over.'

'With the inevitable result?'

'Yes.'

'Many casualties?'

'The gentlemen volunteers were permitted to surrender. As for the rest, we'll never know. This has been a typically Sicilian thing. An insoluble mystery.'

'At all events, we can assume that separatism is dead. What's the local reaction?'

'One of total apathy,' I said.

'That seems to be the case here, too,' the Colonel said. 'Perhaps it's because this happened at a time when all people asked was to be left in peace to get on with their own lives. For them the possession of a sense of history could have been rather a luxury.'

There was a pause, and behind it I sensed a sigh, but not of relief. 'The collapse came rather more rapidly than I'd foreseen,' he said. 'It's to be supposed we'll be moving on fairly soon. Can't see anything to keep us here. I haven't of course spoken to London yet, but I imagine that's what will happen. How are you fixed there? Could you uproot yourself at fairly short notice?'

'I live out of a suitcase.'

'There was some project you were engaged on in your spare time. Something to do with folklore wasn't it?'

'Folk music, in fact.'

'Were you able to do anything with it?'

'Very little as it happened,' I said. 'As it turned out there wasn't much to be done. It was too late.'

'Pity,' he said. 'Sorry to hear that. Still, in that case departure shouldn't be too much of a wrench.'

Something had to be done with the rest of the day, and having nothing to occupy my time I went over to see if anything was happening at the so-called Festival of Truth. I asked Giovanni at the Roma about it, and he said, 'To tell you the truth we've forgotten about that kind of thing. People used to bear grudges and they went there to cut each other up, but that's a thing of the past. Nowadays we live together in peace. There's not much to be seen,' he said, and he was right. There were no stalls and no caravans, and I could see at a glance that this was not the kind of festa where you went to drink or dance, to buy absurd mementos, or to eat bitter cakes. This was a quiet place, too far from anywhere, but in its way it was spell-binding, from another country, Africa perhaps, or a piece of an Arabian desert by the sea. All round, and as far as I could see in any direction, the landscape belonged to the volcano that had kneaded it and padded it and shaped it with its lava, leaving nothing but the soft sweep of old lava fields and here and there a grassy swelling or hump where once there had been ancient crags. But here mysteriously and in utter isolation particles of the ancient Sicily had survived, full of hard and abrupt masses, one being the hillock of uncompromising stone out of which the cave sanctuary of St Angelo a Nilo had been gouged.

After I left the car I had a mile walk along the shore. There were the remains of a road but the sea had washed most of it away. The sea came in a long way, leaving patches of water cut into odd shapes, with herons limping through them and stabbing at the air with their beaks. Over to my right breakers were running at the edge of the tide, and I watched the slow lift of spray into sky as they smashed into the rocks. People were picking their way ahead of me in twos and threes over the slabs of stone and round little pyramids of basalt, making for the shrine.

I climbed a hundred or so steps cut in the rock to reach the flat top where a rough pathway had been hacked out in times long past, smoothed over the centuries by the passage of so many sandalled feet. They kept goats up here in rough enclosures near the shrine, and the smoothed path was slippery where they had splashed it with their urine. A number of middle-aged Sicilians, some clearly married couples, were standing about with nothing apparently to say; just taking in the view. In these country places the usual thing is to greet a stranger, and I was surprised when I said 'good morning' a couple of times and this produced in return only an absent smile. It occurred to me that silences were part of the protocol of the occasion, possibly decided upon as a wise precaution against dangerous truth. All these people were carrying electric torches, from which it was clear that the cave sanctuary was likely to be in near darkness, so on reaching its entrance I held back, and waited for a party to begin the descent before following them down.

The cave was larger and deeper than expected, and the path cut in the rock and protected by an iron hand-rail spiralled one and a half times to reach the bottom. St Angelo a Nilo appeared in a full-length mosaic portrait in a niche, lit by the torches of those who stood before it, motionless and in silence, having come there to pay their respects. This was an accurate portrait of a human being from before the days when Byzantium had applied its graphic formula to distance the gods and saints. St Angelo's face was full of human irregularity, a thin nose, turned a little to one side, one eye a shade lower than the other, the hair rumpled possibly by the saint's hand, in any case wholly free from the precise undulations of the hairstyle of the Monreale patriarchs – or even of Colonel John Simmons. The church images – of which there were many – of St Angelo a Nilo had always been modelled on negroes from the newly discovered black Africa of later days. This man belonged to the times when all that was known of Africa was Alexandria and the Nile and a desert full of lions, and our portrait was of an Alexandrian in a Roman tunic, with a garland of jasmine, a skin blemish on his cheek and the beginnings of a smile probably insisted on by the artist.

I climbed down the rock and began to walk back to where

the car had been left. Small parties of elderly people were coming or going along the shore, walking slowly, reflectively and a little separated from each other. It was a spectacle that filled me with a kind of awe as well as a feeling of loneliness. For three hundred and sixty-four days of the year these people were imprisoned in life's daily deceptions. Here in Sicily, perhaps more than elsewhere, was the magic of truth inaccessible, but on this one day at the beckoning of an African saint they cleansed themselves and worshipped at its shrine. It would have been out of place in passing to wish them *buona festa*, but when I raised my hand in salute they smiled and returned the greeting.

I was attacked by a feeling of impending loss. It was describable as a kind of anxiety to fill in every minute of what was left of time in Palma, to imprint its scenes on the mind, to gather up as a matter of urgency the last of the Sicilian experiences and sensations that would soon be beyond reach. 'When the tree is gone,' says their proverb, with its memory of Arabian sands, 'we appreciate its shade.' This was a preposterous island, but enslaving as well, and I had developed an addiction to its hard flavours, its theatricalities and its restlessness.

Everything had to be salvaged, nothing squandered of these last hours. Running a bath I listened to the throaty outpourings of water brought from some ancient conduit, feeling its coolness flood into every corner of the room, and sniffing its odours of ferns and earth. I pushed open the window and a blade of sunlight sliced through into the room's twilight. The pigeons were clapping their wings in the courtyard, and a girl on a rooftop sang an African song. A car cruised down the street, silently, except for the tyres licking at the tar. I sluiced the cold, fragrant water over myself, dried off hurriedly, and dressed. There were so many papers to be gathered, so many sterile demands, so many claims never to be satisfied, to be stuffed into folders and carried away to some place where they would be forgotten. Locusts had found their way somehow into the building, and were to be swept gently, some of them still twitching, into the corners. After six months traces of pornographic graffiti drawn superbly with the finger-tip in dust remained in high places on the office furniture, and I longed to be able to remove them intact and carry away these Picasso-like masterpieces of erotic art.

A new crack had opened among the tiles in the ground-floor room. I put my ear to it, and after a while imagined that I caught the sound of the earth growling a faint admonition. Even these friendly, familiar earthquake noises were to be filed as part of Sicily in the archives of the mind.

I went in search of Crispi and Moscato, and by good luck found them together in Moscato's room at the museum. Both were in excellent form. In the next day or so General Bugger-all, fulfilled at last by what would be passed off as a butchery, would be on his way back to Milan, carrying Crispi's genealogical chart and certificate which, with the seals affixed by several official bodies, confirmed the General's possession of eight centuries of ancestors, all of them guaranteed to have been irreproachably parasitic. On the strength of the extortionate fees he had extracted for this and the cut-rate pedigrees provided for the junior officers, Crispi was again planning to marry an under-age girl.

'You're deluding yourself, Avvocato,' I told him. 'It will never happen.'

'She's a country lass, unaffected, no pretensions. I'm on a winner this time.'

'Don't you realize the description you've just given us exactly fits your last girlfriend? When will you ever learn?'

'Never, I hope,' Crispi said.

The main reason for their euphoria was a wonderful plot they had hatched together. Despite the original impact made by the mummy sent Moscato by the Prior of the Capuchins in recognition for such votes as he controlled, public interest had quickly flagged. It had been presented as Johnny Walker of whom practically nobody had heard, so now – once again with the complicity of the Prior – small changes were being made to its appearance in an endeavour to attract visitors. Most Sicilians who had gone to school at all had learned something of John Bull, the English agent approached by King Ferdinand's Austrian Queen with an offer to sell the island to the British for six million pounds. What had been agreed was that the Prior would replace the scarlet cutaway coat and grey topper with slightly different garments (although both Walker and Bull belonged roughly to the same period). Johnny Walker, with a Union Jack stuck to his chest, his cheeks painted crimson, and his expression adjusted to register bellicosity rather than despair, would become John Bull. Crispi's part in this trivial deception would be to produce a biographical leaflet for sale to visitors.

'Wasn't the Prior sending you more mummies, doctor?' I asked.

'Of course. We're hoping to receive the next consignment in a matter of days. You can understand there's a bit of a packing problem involved.'

We spent the rest of the afternoon together, sipping the museum's preserving fluid, inspecting the latest crop of antiques looted from Greek tombs, and the fakes the grave-robbers had tried to pass off mixed in with them, and discussing Crispi's marriage prospects. At the end of it I mentioned in a casual way that I would be going. This was the way things were done locally, without warning, in an off-hand fashion. Before taking leave of me at the Roma, Rod and Nancy had fallen upon my neck, thereafter subjecting me to positive re-alignment along with Giuliano and all the other shadows to be dismissed from their memory. Human relationships in this country are stage-managed in a different way. Fatalism holds its great shield over the people. Partings are accompanied by hardly anything more than a word and a clasp of the hand, and whatever is felt is buried. Hundreds of thousands of Sicilian emigrants to the New World turned wordlessly from fathers, mothers, brothers, sisters, even the children who had come with them to the ship, and walked to the gangplank without looking back, thus depriving grief of its gestures. Show nothing, lose nothing, as the saying goes.

Moscato went on scrubbing the clay from a pot made the year before and buried in someone's garden in an attempt to match the patina of antiquity. Crispi added another sentence to his account of the haggling over a price for the island conducted between the agent and the Queen, where only a half million pounds divided the offering price and the price bid. He put down his pen. 'I've come to a decision and I have an announcement to make,' he said. 'As soon as my wife produces an heir I've decided to sell the estate. It's bound to be worth a few thousand lire of anybody's money to be a landowner. We'll come to England to see you. Give us a year – eighteen months at most – and we'll be there.'

With every week that passed my evening walk to the Square seemed to have become longer and less direct. I found more side-turnings to investigate that led me into previously over-looked backwaters of the town, withdrawn and secret places known undoubtedly to everyone but myself, to be incorporated in the continuously expanding promenade. Now, by the clock, it was evening, but although the sun was low in the sky its light was as strong as ever. A recently discovered diversion took me through an orange grove divided by a stream, with red flowers poised like flamingoes along its bank, and the sun's rays pressing through the tight filter of leaves, bathing everything – including the faces of those who strolled there – in deep green light. It shone on jokers on their way to the Gran Paradiso bar, laughing idiot children, women permanently inflated by their overbrimming fecundity, men turned by wealth and self-indulgence into imitation mandarins with inch-long nails on their fingers proving they had never worked, grotto-people of Mediterranean stock that Palma had transformed into Indians. This was the showcase of human adaptability, where morality had never been permitted to interfere with natural selection.

Oranges from the second crop that nobody wanted had fallen from the trees into the stream, and great yellow rafts of them went sliding by on its surface, with goats wading into them, trying with occasional success to snatch up an orange as it passed. The Indians from the grottoes came for the oranges, and a few of them were in the stream competing with the goats, laughing and calling to each other in the high-pitched Andean voices they had developed with their flattened cheek-bones and their barrel chests. The Arch-priest had stopped for a moment to watch this performance on his way to the square, and he was joined by a man carrying an advertisement for a mind-reading show, who dropped first to one knee to kiss his ring. No one, wherever he happened to be going in that part of the town, would fail to come by this way if he possibly could.

Outside the Gran Paradiso a few clowns and poets had already gathered for a brief intake of evening laughter, under the morose gaze of a knot of sufferers from the sadness of the rich, including Inspector Volpe, hoping perhaps to infect themselves with this inexplicable joy. From the Gran Paradiso it was only five minutes to the Cala, a cliff-walled inlet of the sea, full of vapour and spume where old men promenaded stiffly up and down carrying canary birds in cages to benefit their own bronchial tubes and the birds' song by the damp exhalations rising from the water.

In the Square I found every man in his place and every woman out of sight. The undercurrent of public feeling was self-congratulatory and calm, and this in its way was an undeclared celebration. All the delicate adjustments of this society had been thrown off balance, but now things had fallen back into place, and citizens could come here to sit peacefully as they and their fathers before them had always done, lulled and pacified by routine. The miners were back in their mines a thousand yards under the earth. Miraglia was no more. General Bertone, misunderstood and disliked as a foreigner, was on his way to the north leaving a flush of dying prosperity among the shop-keeping classes and a windfall of oil drums to be beaten flat in due course, for conversion into shelters for those who were without houses. By eight o'clock the Easter Island regulars in the Civilized People's Club were all in place. In the background the Archpriest extended a finger to be kissed. Police Marshal Innocente, a late arrival, swept through the door with a swirl of his cloak and a flash of the sword beneath. Minasola, almost invisible as ever, watched with weak eyes from behind a rusted palm brought back in the glorious past as a souvenir from Addis Ababa.

Boys selling newspapers came running into the Square and went into the clubs and round the tables. It was the evening edition of *Corriere* and it had exactly gauged the mood of the occasion. To look for an account of the Niscemesi's supposed obliteration, one had to turn to the back page. The main story, attesting the absolute return to normality, was of an experiment carried out by the newspaper's religious correspondent in collaboration with an independent scientist – a lecturer in physics at the University of Catania – to determine and measure the exact movement of the head of the image of Santa Maria della Vittoria at the occurrence of its annual miracle. This had happened on the previous Sunday when the ivory image had bowed as usual in the direction of the crucifix on the altar. The movement recorded by a series of photographs taken at minute intervals throughout the day, was stated to have been 7.3 mm. A picture of the miraculous event was accompanied by an advertisement for the German camera used in the experiment.

Night came closer in its leisurely and indulgent fashion until it was hard in the contest between light and darkness to decide which had the upper hand. At one moment in this period of contemplation a raised glass was brimful of the rosy reflection of pinnacles and towers, and then – almost between one sip and the next – held nothing but the deep ultramarine of the sky. With this departure of the day (in so far as it could be decided) the great cracked bell in the Church of Santa Maria della Vittoria clanked once. This was the signal for those simple people who were the true repository of faith and (such as it existed at all) hope to slip into bell towers all over the town for two or three tugs on a bell rope, for no other reason than to draw attention to their presence and their needs to listening ears in the sky.

Time to go, I thought. I called the old waiter Giovanni over, wishing to be able to thank him for his solicitude and his service, but unable to do this, because we had become friends, and in Palma a friend was never thanked in words. Instead I put my arm round his shoulder as he leaned over to remove my glass, and he turned on me a rather mournful look as if sensing in this moment of public relaxation and tranquillity that some tiny thing had gone amiss. It seemed to him, however, the moment to mutter in my ear the kind of request one makes to a friend. 'A nephew of mine. He can turn his hand to anything, perhaps if you could write him a recommendation . . .' He waited while I wrote Crispi's name and address on a slip, then handed it to him. Next day I would pop a note to the Avvocato through the old post-office box with most of my remaining lire. 'It's high time somebody weeded that patch of yours, Avvocato. I'm sending a young friend.'

I got up and crossed the Square, stopping for a last glance at a patch of Roman mosaic that had surfaced in it in the course of an earthquake some twenty years before. It was part of an elaborate domestic scene, although not enough of it had been spared by the traffic for an investigator to understand what was going on. Everything in Palma was symbolical of something, but I had always found the vanishing mosaic's symbolism of the blurred faces and arms thrown out in unfathomable gestures to be unusually poignant. A short walk down the alleyway brought me perhaps almost for the last time face to face with the Gulf of Catania in the Ionian sea, which like all other seas possessed features that were remarkable in their own way, in this case subaqueous volcanoes, radiant coral, and cat-eyed fish. The sea was a sheet of slate, its horizons lined as by early stars with the twinkle of fishing lights. Summer lightning that would come to nothing threw bulging, empty clouds into relief. A white rim of water crept within a yard of where I stood, with the faintest of crackling as it invaded the dry sand. The silhouettes of the citizens who had come down here to urinate in silence and dignity were placed like sentinels at the edge of the tide, their backs to the volcano, now a mighty pyramid of cobalt with the day's last flush detained at its tip.

Some hundred yards away the group of Palma's decayed palaces huddled together to await final collapse, appearing in this light like a small isolated cliff, and I set out to walk towards them.

22

Plodding along the shore road it soon became clear that half the town was without light. This was not unusual. Earth subsidences played havoc with underground cables, and further and regular difficulties arose from acts of piracy committed by persons with some knowledge of electrical matters who tapped the company's wiring. For this way they not only stole electricity but frequently caused short-circuits and a loss of supply in affected areas for hours or even days on end.

On the brink of night, the palaces were in darkness, and although I was careful never to go out in the evening without a torch I remembered that the battery in the one I was carrying was low. Down on the beach below the Prizzi Palace the fishermen were busy by the light of a fire. The last of the boats were about to go out. They took an enormous time, working with great method to pile up their nets on the decks, so that they would slip clear and straight down into the depths without risk of entanglement. I watched them for a while at their work, then climbed the beach again and crossed the road to the palace.

I kicked at the gate and waited but was not surprised when there was no sound of movement from within. People left little earthenware lamps with wicks of the most primitive kind all over their houses ready for such emergencies, but everything including matches and oil was in short supply, so that usually when the lights failed they just gave up and went to bed. There being nothing in the palace to steal, security was lax and the chain had been left off, so I lifted the latch, pushed open the gate and went in. I switched on the torch and swung the feeble beam that barely reached the nearest of the cracked walls and arches. For a moment I thought that nothing whatever had been left of the great accumulation of possessions set out here for the benefit of General Bertone and his staff, then the light picked up a single object occupying the exact centre of this desolate space: Garibaldi's stuffed horse, much larger than I had remembered it, glaring back red-eyed into the beam of the torch. The place smelt of hauntings, of abandonment, of moulds gathering on cold stone.

I called out sepulchrally and my voice went charging round the empty spaces. There was a faint creaking of the cabin door on the *galleria* being opened and a moment later the Marchesina materialized at the top of the staircase. She seemed to have wrapped a sheet round herself, and her hair, clouding her features in a misted, untidy fashion, disclosed only a sharp triangle of face. She came slowly down the

228

stairs dangling an oil lamp that illuminated no more than her feet, looking angular and pathetic like a Cruikshank illustration, and hardly larger than a child.

She handed me the lamp then put her arms round me. In this light and without make-up, her mouth had almost disappeared. 'This time you broke all the rules,' she said.

'I had some news,' I said. 'I wanted to be sure of finding you at home.'

'Go on,' she said.

'I'm on my way,' I said.

'When?'

'In a matter of days.'

'Uh huh.'

Even allowing for the Marchesina's background I was slightly hurt at the total absence of reaction. I gestured vaguely at the great emptiness.

'I didn't expect to find the place like this.'

'We only had the furniture for a week. It's up. The horse was too heavy for them to move. He'll be with us a little longer. I'm going to sit down.'

There was a stone bench not more than a foot wide built against the wall and we sat on it. Cruikshank would have been in his element, I thought, but the horse might have been too much for him.

'Wouldn't it be more comfortable upstairs?' I suggested.

'Yes, but we only have one bed left, and it's occupied.'

'Who by?'

'The Seaweed Eater. She sleeps at one end, and I sleep at the other. She's been ill.'

'I can't imagine it. What of?'

'Typhoid. Or so they say. Half our friends were taken ill after the party. They're in hospital in Catania. I had to give the Gallienis my second bed.'

'Were you ill?'

'I've not been at my best. I'm better now.'

'Could it have been the dinner?'

'What else?' she said. 'You're never here when I want you. You might at least carry up some water for me before you go.'

She began to ask a series of inconsequential questions of the kind that Sicilians, who possess little curiosity, employ to pad out a conversation.

'So where did you go tonight?'

'To the Square.'

'Yes, of course, every night to the Square. It's become a necessity. Something you'll miss. And what did you drink?'

'Coffee with acorns. Followed by an amaretto.'

'Having the taste of bitter almonds and death. Who did you see there?'

'The Archpriest, Innocente, Minasola. They were celebrating the end of the separatists. It was more than usually silent.'

'As befits such an occasion,' she said.

'All of them. All the regulars. Allegra who was on trial over the Miraglia affair, Gianturco the baker who mixed earth with his bread, the ex-bandit Sciarpa, the man who worked the big racket in oil and other prime necessities, Canepa who made an estimated five million changing the trademarks on stolen Dunlop tyres, what's-his-name who cuckolded Mussolini, the engineer at the sulphur mine who believes in keeping all the old customs alive, twenty or thirty surplus lawyers and doctors with nothing to do with their lives. And of course the Mayor. I was nearly forgetting the Mayor.'

I suspected that she'd hardly been listening and only the mention of the last personality registered.

'How was he?' she asked absently.

'No better than average. Ten years on Prócida takes its toll. They were all there together enjoying peace at last in their own quiet way.'

'You're there every night. Do you ever see my father?'

'No, and I wouldn't expect to. Not in the Square.'

'Why did he forsake us?' she asked. She was clearly speaking to herself.

The Marchesina pressed the wick further into the lamp, but the oil was nearly used up and the flame was shrinking and burning blue, while my torch when switched on produced no more than a glow in the bulb, and I could barely make out the shape of Garibaldi's horse.

There was a pause and a change in her tone. 'How old are you?' she asked. The question took me by surprise.

'You know perfectly well. Forty.'

'You look much older. Your skin is bad and your muscular tone poor, not to mention other shortcomings. I'm older than you, but which of the two looks the younger?'

'You do, by many years.'

'You travel so much. To me it seems purposeless. Where will you go next?'

'In all probability to the Far East.'

'Do you know why?'

'Not with any certainty.'

'Then change your mind.'

'It's something I've let myself in for.'

'You've little say in your future, is it that?'

'Very little, I suspect. Not much at all.'

'Neither have I. Next year they'll pull the palace down. Next year my father will die. Next year what else? Nothing to laugh about, I'm sure.'

Something moved in the gloom, close to our feet, a rat I suspected.

'The time comes,' she said, 'when we have to look round to see where we can take refuge. It happens to all of us.'

I understood that she had glimpsed the abyss ahead, that she was worn out by the strain of penury stoically faced, by pride's own anguish, abandonments, sickness, and above all the fatigue imposed in the end by too great an appetite for life. At this moment I felt for her nothing but the purest compassion.

Our faces touched in the total darkness. 'I'll be back,' I said. 'Of that you can be sure.'

Arena

☐ The History Man	Malcolm Bradbury	£2.95
☐ Rates of Exchange	Malcolm Bradbury	£3.50
☐ The Painted Cage	Meira Chand	£3.95
☐ Ten Years in an Open Necked Shirt	John Cooper Clarke	£3.95
☐ Boswell	Stanley Elkin	£4.50
☐ The Family of Max Desir	Robert Ferro	£2.95
☐ Kiss of the Spiderwoman	Manuel Puig	£2.95
☐ The Clock Winder	Anne Tyler	£2.95
☐ Roots	Alex Haley	£5.95
☐ Jeeves and the Feudal Spirit	P. G. Wodehouse	£2.50
☐ Cold Dog Soup	Stephen Dobyns	£3.50
☐ Season of Anomy	Wole Soyinka	£3.99
☐ The Milagro Beanfield War	John Nichols	£3.99
☐ Walter	David Cook	£2.50
☐ The Wayward Bus	John Steinbeck	£3.50

Prices and other details are liable to change

ARROW BOOKS, BOOKSERVICE BY POST, PO BOX 29, DOUGLAS, ISLE OF MAN, BRITISH ISLES

NAME. . . . .

ADDRESS . . . .

. . . .

. . . .

Please enclose a cheque or postal order made out to Arrow Books Ltd. for the amount due and allow the following for postage and packing.

U.K. CUSTOMERS: Please allow 22p per book to a maximum of £3.00.

B.F.P.O. & EIRE: Please allow 22p per book to a maximum of £3.00.

OVERSEAS CUSTOMERS: Please allow 22p per book.

Whilst every effort is made to keep prices low it is sometimes necessary to increase cover prices at short notice. Arrow Books reserve the right to show new retail prices on covers which may differ from those previously advertised in the text or elsewhere.